Fearless

Fearless

MANDY GONZALEZ

ALADDIN
New York   London   Toronto   Sydney   New Delhi

ALADDIN

An imprint of Simon & Schuster Children's Publishing Division

1230 Avenue of the Americas, New York, New York 10020

First Aladdin hardcover edition April 2021

Text copyright © 2021 by In This Together Media, LLC and Mandy Gonzalez

Jacket illustrations copyright © 2021 by Geraldine Rodriguez

All rights reserved, including the right of reproduction in whole or in part in any form.

ALADDIN and related logo are registered trademarks of Simon & Schuster, Inc.

For information about special discounts for bulk purchases, please contact Simon & Schuster Special Sales at 1-866-506-1949 or business@simonandschuster.com.

The Simon & Schuster Speakers Bureau can bring authors to your live event. For more information or to book an event contact the Simon & Schuster Speakers Bureau at 1-866-248-3049 or visit our website at www.simonspeakers.com.

Designed by Laura Lyn DiSiena

The text of this book was set in Bookman Old Style.

Manufactured in the United States of America 0221 FFG

10 9 8 7 6 5 4 3 2 1

Library of Congress Cataloging-in-Publication Data

Names: Gonzalez, Mandy, author.

Title: Fearless / by Mandy Gonzalez.

Description: First Aladdin hardcover edition. | New York : Aladdin, 2021. | Series: [Fearless series ; 1] | Audience: Ages 8 to 12. | Summary: While rehearsing what may be the last show in the Ethel Merman Theater, twelve-year-old Monica Garcia and other cast members are locked in and must try to appease a ghost and reverse a curse.

Identifiers: LCCN 2020052779 (print) | LCCN 2020052780 (eBook) | ISBN 9781534468955 (hardcover) | ISBN 9781534468979 (eBook)

Subjects: CYAC: Musical theater—Fiction. | Actors and actresses—Fiction. | Blessing and cursing—Fiction. | Haunted places—Fiction. | Theaters—Fiction. | New York (N.Y.)—Fiction.

Classification: LCC PZ7.1.G6528 Fe 2021 (print) | LCC PZ7.1.G6528 (eBook) | DDC [Fic]—dc23

LC record available at https://lccn.loc.gov/2020052779

LC eBook record available at https://lccn.loc.gov/2020052780

To Doug and Maribelle

One

NEW YORK, NEW YORK

Twenty-four days until opening night

Monica's hand pressed against the window. She could feel it, even before they arrived. *Thump, thump, thump.* She grabbed a strand of her curly brown hair and twisted. "Next stop, Times Square, Forty-Second Street," the automated voice said. Lights flickered through the tunnel as they got closer. Monica twisted faster.

"Tsk-tsk!" her abuelita said, waving her finger from across the aisle at Monica's hair, then went back to studying the subway map on the wall in front of her.

"I can feel it, Abuelita, like your friend said," Monica whispered. Her brown, almond-shaped eyes smiled when she spoke.

The city's heartbeat.

Monica's abuelita's friend had told them that if they wanted to get from JFK Airport to Manhattan, they could take a taxi or a bus or a shuttle. "But if you want to feel the heartbeat of the city under its skin, you take the subway."

"I can feel it too," her abuelita giggled, clutching her purse tighter. She looked out the window and, seeing only blackness, positioned her big circle glasses above the rim of her nose—the same pair of glasses she'd owned since the 1970s. How she was ever able to manage keeping those thick glasses in place on her slender face all these years, no one knew.

The subway braked hard and slowed. Monica's abuelita startled, and her back went straight. "This is Times Square, Forty-Second Street," the automated voice said now. Monica lifted herself out of her seat to get a better look. The panels of walls and lights and spaces in between made patterns as they glided by. At that moment, Monica was thinking how incredible it was that two people could find their way from all the way across the country to this very spot at this very moment and enter into an entirely new world, just like that! Travel had always seemed to her like something other people did.

Standing riders in the train wiggled to make room for

Monica as she stood up, and then an entire subway car crammed with people all instinctively leaned in the same direction to balance themselves as the subway hit its brakes entering the station. Monica wobbled and grabbed the one small piece of hand space left on the center pole, and she leaned too. This made her want to burst into tears of joy. She was leaning into New York City, she thought, and laughed.

As the train rolled to a stop, a man with a deep voice at the rear of the subway car shouted, "Welcome to paradise," and the doors opened. Monica's abuelita got up and poked her head out of the subway car. Lifting her luggage, she said to her granddaughter, "Oh, and look at the view!"

"It's amazing!" Monica replied, wide-eyed. A crowd of impatient passengers pushed their way past the two awe-struck tourists, getting out of the crowded car as fast as possible.

As they hurried out of the train and onto the platform, they saw two men energetically beating on plastic buckets with drumsticks and hollering an occasional "Hoot ho!" Monica's abuelita told her the subway station was over one hundred years old. But all Monica could think of was how new everything seemed, and all this newness gave her a melty feeling.

Another train arrived on a different track, releasing

more people onto the platform. A tall woman with a red face and a fancy-looking tote bag bumped into Monica and with a stern "pardon me" rounded past her, knocking her off balance. She fumbled and got swept up into a crowd of people moving at different speeds, and she became so turned around and pushed to the side, she realized she couldn't see her abuelita anymore.

The commuter crowd moved in a fever past her, and then the platform quieted. Thankfully, she now saw that her abuelita was right next to her.

"Elbows out!" her abuelita hollered.

They got swept up in more crowds, heading toward the exit—like fish going upstream. Monica still couldn't believe she was on New York City soil. This was incredible for two reasons: one, she'd never even been out of the state of California before; and two, she'd never thought she'd get out of the state of California ever. The drumming stopped. She inhaled deeply and let out a quiet "Meeeee." She held the note just long enough for it to vibrate gently. The sound echoed softly down the dark tunnel, and it came as somewhat of a relief. Her location had changed, but her singing voice was the same. She inhaled again to take in the smells of this new world. She had so hoped New York would smell like cotton candy, but it most certainly did not.

Her abuelita was now leading the way, showing her with body language how to weave through the crowds. The big white feather on her abuelita's hat flounced as she walked. Her abuelita insisted this was the kind of hat you wore only to church and to New York City. Besides the hat, Monica's abuelita wore purple yoga pants, black Converse sneakers, and a leopard-print backpack. Some might have described Monica's abuelita as avant-garde.

They passed through station doors covered in advertisements and stickers and landed in an enormous sea of people and lights. They were blanketed by a million stories being told at once, and that offered Monica a certain sense of tranquility. So much cement and steel, and yet she was certain she'd just tumbled into a bed of wildflowers. Even in broad daylight, the lights of the city outshone the sun in rainbow colors. Lights so welcoming they made even the dirty sidewalks sparkle.

"Which one is the Empire State Building?" Monica's abuelita asked. She pointed to one building, then another. "That one? No. That one? No. That one? No." She laughed. "They all look tall!" Then she laughed again when she looked over at Monica and saw her expression.

Directly in front of Monica was a billboard advertising soup with actual steam coming out of the bowl. She'd seen it so many times in photographs, and now it was there in real life, steam billowing like the incense Father Mendez would wave above her head on Sundays. It was beautiful. And the sequin ball that dropped on New Year's Eve was high above that. *It* was beautiful. Billboards for Broadway musicals and advertisements for shoes and perfume and watches all moved at different speeds. All beautiful! And all hers to behold in that moment.

Suddenly a person dressed in an Elmo costume towered over her, blocking her view. He had a stitched-on smile. Monica smiled back. Elmo waved to Monica without saying a word. She waved back without saying a word. He handed her a flyer for dishwashers being sold at deep discount prices and then moved on. She studied the flyer, a little disappointed it wasn't something more exciting, and passed the flyer to her abuelita, who hugged it, then placed it in her purse. "We might need a dishwasher. You never know," she laughed.

A few more steps and a man leaned in toward them asking for spare change. Monica's abuelita dug a few quarters out of her purse and placed them in the man's empty Styrofoam coffee cup. "Have a blessed day, young lady," he said to her abuelita. Monica's abuelita grabbed the top of her hat, lifted her chin in the air, and giggled like a schoolgirl. It was official: Monica Garcia was in love with New York City.

"Did you ever think four weeks ago we'd be in New York City?" Monica's abuelita said, rummaging for more change to give out.

New York City had been the furthest thing from Monica's mind when she'd gotten called out of her seventh-grade science class by Mrs. Drury, the school's secretary, less than a month ago. They'd been measuring the length of Peter Davis's forearm and comparing it to the size of a dinosaur tooth when the knock came on the classroom door. Mrs. Drury kept repeating it was an "urgent phone call for Miss Garcia," but then she made Monica walk very slowly down the hall to the principal's office.

"Even urgent phone calls don't give one permission to run in the halls," she said with her usual pinched expression. Monica had known Mrs. Drury since kindergarten, and she'd never, not even once, not even during the school talent-show comedy routines, seen her without a pinched look on her face.

"What kind of urgent phone call, Mrs. Drury?" Monica asked anxiously.

"Oh, I'm not one to say, nor do I think I even know," she said as she casually walked past lockers and display windows with a feather duster. Mrs. Drury dusted things when she walked, like some people chewed gum.

"Is the call from my mother?" Monica implored. Why

did science class have to be at the very, very far end of the school when a very important phone call came in?

"From your mother? Oh yes, yes. It's urgent." Mrs. Drury was hardly paying attention to the signs of Monica's growing anxiety. She was more concerned with the dust bunnies that had collected on the trophy shelves.

When they finally got to the principal's office and opened the door, the first person Monica saw was her father.

"Papí?"

Things were worse than she'd thought. Her father never left the crop fields, especially during high picking season. This time of year it was olives. He was the foreman and had to make sure everything ran smoothly, so she wasn't certain how he had been able to sneak away.

His tanned skin still had beads of sweat from the hot sun, and his work boots were caked with soft wet mud. He was rubbing the lucky rabbit's foot on his keychain.

Then her mother came around the corner into the office, having just thrown away a tissue from wiping her tears.

"Mamí?" Monica said, and rushed into her arms. Now she knew something was terribly wrong. Like her dad, her mother worked long hours in the farm office, handling the paperwork and logistics. And with the busy season, they were both always, well . . . busy. "Is it Freddy?"

"Monica. They called," her mom said through more tears and then a smile.

Monica was confused.

"They called!" her mother repeated with laughter.

"Who called?"

Her father removed his cowboy hat and wiped sweat from his brow. He said in his usual gentle voice, "Broadway called, Kita."

Monica's first reaction should have been excitement. But she was completely petrified.

She and her parents sat in the parking lot of the school in their SUV.

"What exactly did the voicemail say?" Monica asked her mother.

"She just said to call her back as soon as we got the message," Monica's mother said. "We couldn't wait until after school." Her mother, still wearing her jeans and a bandanna around her neck, pulled a phone number out of her pocket, pursed her lips, and pushed it into Monica's hand.

Monica looked at the phone number. A New York area code. Then she thought of Lucy Sanchez. Lucy was in Acting Club with Monica at school. Orange Grove Middle

School didn't have much in the way of a performing arts program, just two small productions a year held in the cafeteria. "Don't get your hopes up," Lucy had said to Monica when she'd overheard Monica telling Marissa she'd made an audition tape. "Kids from Orange Grove don't make it to Broadway."

Marissa and Monica had been best friends since before they could crawl. Their parents worked on the farm together. If there was anyone on the entire planet who understood Monica, it was Marissa. And vice versa. They called themselves the M&M's. "Don't listen to Lucy," Marissa had said. "She only wishes she had your voice."

"Can't you call for me?" Monica asked her mother.

"No, she wants to talk to you. Call her Ms. Roy when she answers."

Helen Roy was the New York casting director for the much-anticipated Broadway show *Our Time*, a musical homage to classic 1980s adventure movies.

Monica dialed the number nervously. The casting director picked up right away.

"Hello, Ms. Roy? This is Monica Garcia. . . ." Monica's voice cracked.

"Hello, Monica. I'm glad you were able to call me back today." Her voice was soothing. "Actors will say that you'll hear from a casting director anywhere between an hour and a year after an audition." Ms. Roy let out a little laugh. "But we'd like to move quickly on this one, as you can imagine. We need to nail down our entire cast right away, especially the children's parts, since there are school obligations to consider."

Monica nodded before saying quietly, "Yes, I understand."

"The producers and director were very impressed with your video audition."

"Oh, thank you," Monica said, smiling at her mother. Her father clasped the rabbit's foot and rubbed anxiously.

"Usually we like to see actors in person, but we really got a good sense of your style through your tape. Thank you for that. You brought to the performance what we want to see in the character Tony."

Monica's eyes lit up. Tony was one of the leads in the show.

Her mother grabbed Monica's arm and held in tears.

"However," she continued, "we feel you still need a little more coaching and experience. Do you understand?"

Monica paused. Her shoulders slumped. She looked at her parents with sad eyes.

"Yes, I understand." She had prepared for the bad news even before she placed the call. *Kids from Orange Grove don't make it to Broadway.*

"We have the leads already lined up. . . ." Ms. Roy paused, sensing Monica's disappointment. "Yet we'd like to give you an opportunity to get a *taste* of Broadway"—her voice held on the word taste—"as an understudy. Get your feet wet a little. So, if you're okay with that—"

Monica lit up. "Yes! Yes I'm okay with that," she said, bubbling with excitement.

Ms. Roy laughed. "Good, then. I'll have my assistant call and work out the details with you and your parents soon. We'll see you on Broadway, Monica!"

The phone went dead.

"Understudy." Monica smiled. Her parents gave out a joyous cry and raised their hands in the air. Climbing trees, shaking branches full of olives, and gathering the small fruits from the tarp had worn them down. Farming was a tough job.

"I owe Freddy a jelly doughnut. He won the bet." Monica smiled, looking at California's Sierra Nevada in the distance.

Monica pulled out her phone and took a quick photo of the street scene and texted it her parents: New York, New York! For the fourth time that day, there was no response. No response when she'd called to say they'd landed safely at the airport, no response when she'd texted a photo of her abuelita standing next to a man they were convinced was a famous actor outside the airport. No response when she'd texted to say it wasn't actually a famous actor, and no response now. Her parents always got back to her right away. Maybe it was the three-hour time difference. The sun was just starting to rise out west. It could be that.

Monica watched as her abuelita raised her hand to hail a cab. She called out over the din of the bustle. Taxi after taxi raced past without stopping.

"Twenty thousand streets in New York City full of cabs, and I can't catch one?"

Monica shook her head.

"Abuelita, you know our hotel is only a couple blocks away." And because they hadn't packed much—they were used to living with very little—their luggage wasn't much of a burden.

Her abuelita shrugged and said, "I know. I've just always wanted to hail a New York yellow."

They started to move in the direction of their hotel. Monica, who had been absorbed in the scenery, stopped in her tracks. She grabbed her abuelita's arm and pointed upward. Her mouth hung open. In bright neon lights was the billboard for *Our Time*. Her production in lights! A new wave of excitement came over her: "Abuelita! Look!"

Monica's abuelita clapped her hands together. "Oh, Kita!"

"Can we see the Ethel Merman Theater before we check in to our hotel? It's only a few more blocks. *Please?*"

Monica's abuelita thought about the promise she had made to Monica's mother nine hours earlier to go straight to the hotel. "No sightseeing!" Monica's mother had said. "This is a work trip." All understudies were due at rehearsal at eight o'clock sharp the next morning, and with the time difference, Monica would be jet-lagged and tired. She would need to rehearse her lines. Her voice needed to be rested. They had taken the red-eye because it was cheapest, but it wasn't the most accommodating for anyone's sleep schedule. Or a singer's voice.

"Please, Abuelita!" Monica begged. "We can be quick!"

Her abuelita responded with a clap. "I have waited sixty-seven years to see New York. Why waste time napping in a hotel?"

Monica and her abuelita turned their course toward the theater, startling a flight of pigeons. Her abuelita looked at Monica and said, like a sailor with a New York accent, "Hey, why don't ya look where you're goin'. You'd think it was your first time in New York." Monica started to laugh. She recognized the line right away. It was from the opening scene of one of their favorite musicals, the classic production *On the Town*. Monica responded with the next line of the scene, saying in a goofy voice: "It is! It is!" Monica and her abuelita did a little dance, right there in the street. And Monica couldn't believe she was actually dancing . . . on Broadway!

Two

CARRIED AWAY

When Monica and her abuelita arrived at the old Ethel Merman Theater, a small, ornate building tucked away in a charming historic neighborhood just on the edge of Broadway, they saw something they weren't expecting at all: an ambulance out front with its doors open and its lights going.

"What is going on?" Monica wondered. She saw that a dark-haired girl about her age was being wheeled out of the theater on a stretcher. She had a neck brace, and her right leg was wrapped in ice.

As she was lifted into the ambulance, she let out a helpless moan in a tone that frightened Monica. A slender man with wild gray hair followed closely behind. He spoke frantically to the ambulance driver, repeatedly saying, "How could this happen? How could this happen?"

The ambulance driver looked at him blankly and said, "You tell me," then handed him paperwork.

The man signed the paperwork and continued, "It doesn't make sense. None of this makes any sense! How, just tell me how!"

The ambulance driver shrugged his shoulders, "Look, you wanna have tea together and talk about life and its many hazards, or you want me to get this kid to the hospital?"

Monica and her abuelita looked at each other. The wild-haired man threw up his hands and told the driver to go. Then he noticed Monica standing there with her luggage and fresh face. Monica rubbed her ear.

"Can I help you?" he asked. His demeanor abruptly changed.

"Maybe?" Monica said with surprise, feeling self-conscious about her messy hair and unfashionable travel outfit. She gave a hint of a smile.

"You look familiar. . . . What's your name . . . ?" He snapped his fingers, trying to remember how he knew her face.

"Monica," she said quietly.

"Monica! Yes, Monica. Monica what . . . ?" His snaps got tighter and faster as he grew impatient.

"Monica Garcia?" She reached for her hair and started twisting. Her abuelita gave her a swift tap to stop.

"You sing and write songs. Your audition video. Yes, yes, I remember you now. Very good."

Monica blushed.

"You're the understudy to the understudy for our show!"

"An understudy for the understudy?" Monica asked. She didn't even know such a thing existed.

"For the understudy of Tabitha Fox." he said, trying to clarify things.

The doors on the ambulance closed.

"Tabitha Fox is out of the production, and"—he pointed to the ambulance—"*that* was Tabitha's understudy. "Since you're here, why don't you come in and see what you're getting yourself into? Get changed," he said, slicking back his mussed hair with one hand. "You're in."

He started to walk back into the theater, then paused for a moment.

He tapped the script on her head gently and said, "Welcome to Broadway, kid." He turned back inside the theater just as abruptly as he'd come out.

The ambulance rolled away slowly without its lights on, and Monica and her abuelita were left staring at the entrance of the Ethel Merman Theater in disbelief.

"That was Artie Hoffman," her abuelita said.

Monica said, "He's a lot older than I thought he'd be." Her abuelita responded, "And he's a lot younger than I thought he'd be." They turned to each other and smiled.

Famed director Artie Hoffman, known for his plot twists and experimentation with art form, was considered the wild child of Broadway royalty. "People revere him and fear him" was how the casting director's assistant had described him over the phone to Monica.

It was a highly publicized story when Artie Hoffman announced he'd be directing a big production at the tired little Ethel Merman Theater. People loved a comeback story. The last few years hadn't been kind to Artie, and *Our Time* was going to change all that. "Did they think I was just going to go away?" he was quoted as saying. "I have four Tony Awards and a street in Ohio named after me."

"What are you waiting for? Get inside," Monica's abuelita said with a gentle nudge. Monica stayed glued to the pavement.

"I'm not ready," Monica said, reaching for the elephant necklace that was usually around her neck. But it wasn't there. She had left her good-luck charm back in California.

"Come on, you can do this." The feather bobbed on her abuelita's hat, adding punctuation.

Monica stammered, "I—I can't go in there. We just got

here. I'm human lasagna." She waved her hands over her wardrobe.

Earlier they had joked about having to dress in layers for the long journey from West Coast to East Coast. The plane would be cold; New York would be milder; the subway would be hot. Monica had a rain jacket on over her sweater over her overalls, and a thin, old T-shirt underneath that. Plus, her long curly hair had gone limp and straight from the weather. If her brother had been there, he'd have called her Pancake Head. He was ten, the age when you can still get away with saying cute stuff, but you know you're walking a thin line.

"Here, here. Give me your jacket and sweater." Her abuelita helped Monica shed a few clothes and then quickly pulled a comb out of her purse and tidied up her hair. Her hair now looked worse. "You look like a lead to me. Go!"

"Aren't you coming with me?"

"Do you really want your abuelita with you?"

Yes and no.

"You will be fine, Kita."

"Here, in case of emergency." She handed Monica a twenty-dollar bill. "For a cab if you need it, or lunch."

"Why would I need a cab?"

"You never know. . . ." With that, Monica's abuelita

grandly leaned out into the street, and with a loud whistle, the kind you do using your fingers, she got the attention of a taxi, grabbed the luggage, and was gone.

As Monica was about to walk through the front door of the theater, her phone rang.

"Mamí!" Monica said with relief.

"Oh, Monica! I'm so sorry." Her mom sounded tired.

"Guess where I am, Mamí! Right outside the Ethel Merman!"

Monica noted the long silence that followed. Her mother was not one for long silences.

"Honey, you need your rest before tomorrow." Her mother's voice was raw and scratchy. Monica could tell she had been crying.

"Is everything okay? Is Freddy okay?" Monica asked.

Another long silence.

Her brother, Freddy, was three years younger. Gangly, with two dimples and a large cowlick that made a section of his mop of black hair stand up straight at all times. He hated his cowlick as much as Monica loved it. Once, he'd even tried hairspray to mat it down. Another time, he convinced Monica to cut it off with a pair of kitchen scissors, so she did. Though of course it grew back, same as before.

"Mamí, what's wrong with Freddy?"

There was a pause, then a sigh. It had been easier to

avoid the truth when Monica was younger, but now that she was older, things were too apparent to keep from her any longer.

"He had another episode."

Monica's view of the Ethel Merman Theater went blurry. She'd begun to hate the word "episode." Nothing good came from that word. Freddy had been having episodes since he was two years old. The first one had happened on Christmas Eve. He spiked a fever and the seizures began. Christmas gifts lay under the tree, still wrapped, for days. The episodes got more and more frequent and went from being a surprise to being part of their regular world.

"Was this one bad, Mamí?"

"Kita, you have bigger things to think about right now." Her mother tried to sound comforting.

"Tell me the truth. Was this one bad?" Monica demanded.

A pause. Her mother sighed again.

"Yes, this one was bad. Oh, our sweet principito." Little prince. Monica's abuelita had given him that nickname. The joke was that Freddy could do no wrong and was loved by anyone who met him.

Dr. Wallace had said that if he kept having more serious seizures he would need to have surgery. Monica didn't really understand it—all she knew was that they'd have to put Freddy to sleep for a few hours and implant some kind of device inside his head to stimulate the nerves or something. She also knew that for her parents, that kind of surgery would cost a lot of money and was completely out of the question. But maybe not so out of the question if she was a success on Broadway.

"Sweetheart, Freddy is resting and fine. Let's find a better time to talk about this. Not when you're standing in front of the Ethel Merman Theater about to start your new life."

Monica hung up with a pit in her stomach.

Just then her phone pinged. It was a text from Marissa.

You in NYC, Mo?

Monica thought before she responded. She didn't want to give her best friend too much hope.

Just got in, Monica texted back.

I want to hear evvvveerryyything!!! That was followed by smiley emojis, followed by Break a leg, followed by I'm soooo jelly! Monica texted back a big red heart.

Monica looked at the big, heavy doors of the Ethel Merman. She took a deep breath and walked into her new life.

Three

TWENTY THOUSAND BEADS OF LIGHT

Inside, the theater was dark and still. Artie Hoffman was nowhere to be found. Monica followed the lights and faint sounds of voices coming from the main auditorium. She walked through a bank of doors, and the theater spread out before her. Her eyes went big. It had seemed so small from the outside, but it was huge! Red and gold velvet-flock wallpaper lined each wall. Statues made of marble looked down at the stage in frozen expressions, and a grand center chandelier, twenty thousand beads of low light, created a gentle glow. Monica had spent many hours performing in community theaters, but nothing came even close to *this*. As she went down the rows, though, she noticed that the seat cushions were worn, and the beautiful wallpaper couldn't hide the large cracks in the walls, and the place smelled musty.

Onstage stood the world-famous choreographer Maria Marquez. Monica blinked twice. Could it be? Even from the back of the auditorium she looked six feet tall. She had heard Maria was doing the choreography for the show, but she'd never thought she'd actually meet her.

"Are you the *new* new Tabitha?" Maria asked loudly.

Monica couldn't believe she was actually talking to her. Was she talking to her?

Maria, in an all-black outfit, walked with a long, elegant stride and perfect posture to the lip of the stage. She had the spotlight.

The three other child actors onstage turned to look at her.

Monica nodded shyly. Her stomach fluttered.

"Well, that was quick," Maria said. "Good. I like punctual."

"You know this theater eats kids for lunch," said a boy with jet-black hair sitting on the floor at the front of the stage as if he had nothing left to give.

"Great, scare the *new* new girl," said a slender, dark-haired girl about Monica's age.

"Well, she wasn't here for the whole 'waterfall saga,'" the boy said, using air quotes. "We should probably catch her up. And give her full-body armor." He coiled gum around his finger.

"No, *no*. What did I say about gum!" Maria stomped.

They all stared at Monica again. Stage left, Monica noticed what looked like a tank of water with perhaps a waterfall feature in mid-construction and yellow caution tape around it. Otherwise the stage was empty of props or backdrops.

"Hi, I'm Relly." A bright, smiling boy with electric-blue hair and pink ballet slippers sat cross-legged on the floor, waving a flashlight.

Monica didn't know what to say, so she waved awkwardly and nervously said, "I . . . I'm Monica."

"I'm Hudson," the larger boy on the floor said with a casual wave.

"And I'm April!" The girl waved with enthusiasm.

"Well, let's not waste any time. Come down, come down. Let's take a good look," said Maria.

Monica walked down a side aisle. The carpeting felt wet and squishy under her feet. The place was musty, with almost the same smell as the pond near the farm where her parents worked. Every step she took, she felt more and more ridiculous in her overalls. They made a rough rubbing sound. It was all anybody heard as she walked. Then her Adidas tennis shoes started making a noise every step. Maybe it was just loud to her.

"You're loud, for a quiet girl," Hudson commented.

Nope, *everyone* could hear it.

"I will not permit you to dance in those shoes," Maria said.

The twenty-dollar bill burned in her pocket. Maybe she could catch a cab back to JFK. For a split second she stopped and turned to leave. There was still time.

Maria stopped her. "No, *no*. The stage is this way, my dear."

She turned back around and continued. The longest twenty paces of her life. She walked almost to the foot of the stage as everyone stared.

"You're tall," said Maria rubbing her chin. "What do I do with tall?"

It had taken Monica her entire childhood to come to terms with being "the tall girl." Fortunately for her, nothing tall rhymed with Monica. Even a harmonica held vertically was pretty short. One time a scrawny boy had called her the Tower in gym class, but it had never stuck. She was glad for that.

"And is this how you dress for dance rehearsal?"

"Well . . . uh . . . I just got off the—"

"I have something that will fit you!" April said, jumping up eagerly from the floor.

April was petite with long brown hair pulled back from her pretty face in a smooth, high, straight ponytail. She had theater eyes, as Monica's abuelita would say—eyes that were so expressive they spoke without words. She was maybe a year younger than Monica, short for her age. But big-tiny. Big personality, tiny body. That type.

"Yes, yes"—Maria waved her off—"you can take five . . . why not. Another five, everyone." She threw her hands in the air and walked off the stage.

April led Monica down a narrow hall and up a couple of flights of stairs, talking the whole time. She clearly knew her way around the theater. "Here's the wig room. You'll love Chris. He gets wigs made from actual people hair. People from Europe, so probably nobody's hair you know." She blew past too quickly for Monica to lean in. "The director's room—door's *always* closed—and the sound room . . . door's *always* open." A man in the middle of telling a joke was roaring like a lion as another man laughed and waved a hankie at him.

The men stopped what they were doing and waved. Monica waved back. April looked at the men laughing, then looked at Monica and laughed as well. As uncomfortable as Monica felt, having interrupted their rehearsal, April made her feel welcome. "Studio A"—a group of adult actors were mid-rehearsal. "Studio B"—more actors.

"That's ensemble—hardest-working people on the stage."

April was going at lightning speed. "They make leads like us look good." April smiled.

Monica had never thought of herself as a lead before. She was usually ensemble.

Different rooms had different groups of people, all doing something together but separate from the other rooms. As they got deeper into the theater, Monica noticed oddities. Back here definitely wasn't as grand as the main stage. A wall made entirely of unpainted plywood, a coconut-size hole in the floor. Crews were fixing and patching everywhere. Nothing seemed finished. A bucket placed under a leaking pipe. Big strips of duct tape over cracks. Monica looked closely at a shelf. Was that . . . mouse poop? As beautiful as the auditorium was, backstage was slightly unnerving. And disappointing.

"Relly Morton, the kid onstage with the blue hair . . . total triple threat. Kind of kid who falls off chairs laughing. Relly hasn't had much formal training, but his natural talent is astounding. He's made to be on Broadway. Even his eyelashes were made for Broadway. Might be the smallest one out there, but he has the highest fan kick." April made herself laugh. "It's true. He's perfect to play the role of Pax—he is curious about everything."

April was still talking when they entered her dressing room.

"Hudson Patel. He's the bigger one sitting on the floor. Cast as Crash. Two left feet, and funniest guy ever. Hmm . . . and sarcastic. His parents moved here from India when Hudson was a baby. You might recognize him"—Monica looked at her blankly—"because not only has he had some roles off-Broadway, but he has an online cooking show with like a million followers. So we'll eat well. Oh! This is my dressing room. I share it with Tabitha."

They looked at each other.

"I guess this is *our* dressing room now?" April said, more slowly.

She pulled out her phone and took a quick selfie of the two of them. "I hope you don't mind. I have a lot of Insta followers who like to see what life is like behind the scenes. You know!" Monica noticed she was already posting it with the hashtag *#newroomie*.

The dressing room had been decorated like a bedroom in a teen magazine—without the bed. Two fuzzy pink chairs faced each other with a trunk between them, string lights, a bubble-gum machine, and stuffed animals. Posters hung on walls from Broadway shows April had performed in—"six, to be exact." *Annie, Matilda, Aladdin, Little Red, Les Misérables, Into the Woods.*

The community theaters Monica was used to only had common dressing rooms with separate changing areas.

Sometimes there were twelve to fifteen actors in one dressing room. She studied the posters on the walls; then her focus turned to a delicate, pastel, diamond-shaped yarn weaving April had hung over the corner of her dressing-room mirror. April was busy digging in Tabitha's trunk for clothes.

"Honestly," she said as she rummaged, "None of my things will fit you. I'm short. And you're *really* tall. How tall are you? But Tabitha's clothes will. She was pretty tall. Her understudy didn't even last two weeks. I mean, that won't happen to you or anything. I have a good feeling about you. You don't stumble over yourself. Do you stumble over yourself?"

April paused to take a breath and noticed Monica looking at the diamond-shaped yarn sculpture.

"It's a god's eye," April said. Monica turned her full attention to April. April threw her some clothes to rehearse in. "Made it at summer camp a few years ago. This horrible, horrible all-girls camp in upstate New York. Have you ever been to upstate New York? It's really pretty. Where are you from, anyway?" April set down a bunch more clothes on Tabitha's—Monica's—dressing table.

"California," Monica said softly.

April continued, "Oh, California! I don't know if you have these in California, but in upstate New York they have enormous lakes with these loons that sound like they're laughing with rubber bands stuck in their throats." She imitated the call. "Eerie but pretty, right? But the camp . . . awful! All the girls hated me. . . . Same day I made the god's eye, I got the lead in *Into the Woods* on Broadway and it became my good-luck charm. Some people say this theater is cursed, so"—she shrugged her shoulders—"why not give yourself a little protection in that department? Insurance. You know what I mean. Oh! My last name is DaSilva, by the way. April DaSilva. You might have heard of me? Ha! I was actually born in May. Weird, I know. I play Froggie. I'm sure that doesn't surprise you."

April offered her an oddly professional handshake. Monica shook her hand quietly.

Monica had promised her abuelita she would not be shy. Her awkward silences made people uncomfortable. Monica could perform in front of hundreds of people, but felt uncomfortable with just one person. But it looked like April wasn't too bothered. She saw the power in Monica's silence. Or maybe she just had a lot to say.

"Would you like to see something . . . ?" Monica asked shyly, digging through her backpack.

"What?" April was curious.

Monica pulled out a similar diamond-shaped weaving from her backpack. Hers was made of smooth wheat reeds and woven much tighter. *"Ojo de Dios,"* Monica finally said, in a voice that was gentle but strong.

April's eyes widened, and her mouth opened in shock.

"God's eye," Monica translated for April. "They are said to have the power to see what we cannot." Monica held the matching god's eye up toward April's. The two girls smiled at each other. "Insurance," Monica repeated.

They both laughed again, more comfortable with each other now.

"So what happened to Tabitha?" Monica asked.

"One day she was here and the next day, *poof*!" April said, shaping her hands like fireworks.

"Poof?" repeated Monica.

"Who leaves two weeks into rehearsal? She said this place gave her the creeps. Said she saw something onstage late one night."

"Like what kind of something?" Monica trembled.

April ignored the question. "Personally? Stays between us?" April gave Monica a serious look. Monica nodded. "I think whatever it was, Tabitha was faking it."

Monica had to think about that for a second. "Why?"

April ignored the question again. Then she decided to answer it: "She probably thought this show was going to be a flop, like all the other shows at the Ethel Merman, and she didn't want her name attached to a flop. *People*," April said with a huff. "And now we have less than a month left of rehearsal time until opening night."

Monica had to process that. Then a wave of panic washed over her, but she forced a nervous smile.

"So, how many Broadway productions have you been in?" April asked. "We could take down Tabitha's posters and put yours up."

Monica looked at the wall of Tabitha's posters, which were way more than April's, and just continued to smile.

Four

CENTER OF BALANCE

When Monica and April returned to dance rehearsal, a new person was standing on the stage. April grabbed Monica's arm. "Don't freak out, but that's Hugh Lavender!"

"Who's Hugh Lavender?" Monica whispered, not freaking out.

"'Who's Hugh Lavender?'" April squealed. "Hugh Lavender is *only* one of the most famous doctors on TV! *Beverly Hospital*?" Monica shrugged. "You've never watched *Beverly Hospital*?" Monica's family didn't watch much television.

Hugh looked exactly liked you'd imagine a famous TV doctor looking. Tall, chiseled, with sandy hair, and piercing blue eyes that caught the light just right. His confident posture revealed that he seemed to be quite aware of exactly how striking he was. Artie and Hugh were childhood friends. It was no coincidence he had put his television career on hold for a few months to give Broadway a try. Was he perfectly cast as the rat-faced lead bad guy, Patrick Murphy? No. A little too. . . pretty. Could he outdance anyone in an audition? Absolutely not. But he was Hugh Lavender. "I've always wanted to play a bad guy," Hugh had said with a soapy wink and a smile when Artie gave him the part. Most important, Hugh Lavender's name looked good in marquee lights outside the theater. Artie's show would draw in the crowds with a name like that. It was the perfect plan.

"This is a barrel," Maria said as she rolled out a large brown barrel. "This barrel will be your best friend in the chase scene." She went to the wing of the stage and rolled out another barrel.

"Welcome back, ladies. Much better attire, new Tabitha."

"Her name is not new Tabitha. It's Monica. From California," April stated.

"Fine then, Monica from California . . . you'll be sitting out today, but you will be warming up and taking notes from the house."

Monica looked down at her dance outfit. April shrugged.

Relly went over and stood next to one of the barrels. It came up past his chest.

"These puppies are big." He leaned in. It was hollow but for one wooden step inside to stand on.

"There's a lot of fightography in this scene," April whispered to Monica. "Maria's brought in a special fight coach for us. It can get aggressive onstage, but you should be fine."

Monica was a little nervous about that.

From what Monica knew from the script she had read, *Our Time* was about four friends—Tony, Froggie, Pax, and Crash—trying to figure out how to save their local arcade, the Tilt, from being bulldozed and turned into a luxury hotel. The kids decide the only way to save the Tilt is to find a treasure thought to have been hidden in caves in the woods behind Tony's house, and use it to buy the Tilt's building and games back. The first act took place in a typical suburban neighborhood. But in act two, the set was magically transformed into dark woods with an underground cave.

Throughout the show, there were a lot of comical dance routines. A lot of chases. There was an actual tomato fight onstage, and an actor pulling the fire alarm of the theater. Glow-in-the-dark foam noodles came out. The highlight and central piece of the set was a fifteen-foot waterfall with real water that the kid actors would slide down in the middle of a scene where the villainous hotelier chased them. Monica hoped she'd get a chance to try it. If the stage crew could get the waterfall to work, that is.

There was a set that looked like an underground cave that was able to be moved to float above the stage when the stagehands pulled the ropes from the fly rails off stage right. Special gears had been designed to rotate a platform as scenes changed. It was an elaborate set, with a lot of complicated choreography. And that meant there was a lot that could go wrong.

The chase scene that Monica was watching happened in act two of the show. It was one of the harder routines.

"Now," said Maria. "During this scene, each one of you will at some point climb into a barrel, climb out of a barrel, hide behind it, race in front of it, and be its dance partner. That's when Hugh and his gang come in." Hugh took a bow. "You following?" Maria rolled out two more barrels. Four total, one for each child character.

"The scene opens with Froggie. April, you're here." She positioned her at one of the front barrels. Relly, you're there. Hudson, you and Monica from California will be at the back barrels." They got into position except for Monica. Maria stood in her spot.

"April, you will jump onto the overturned barrel to

provoke the bad guys. You three will use your barrels to block the bad guys' lunges. Got it?"

They did leap after leap and turn after turn, over and over again. "Stop!" Maria would interrupt. "Flexibility—where is your flexibility!" She would call out, "You are not a brick wall. Keep up, keep up." Monica pulled out her black-and-white composition notebook and took notes. She took her notebook everywhere with her. She had dozens of notebooks at home filled with lyrics and ideas for songs, poems she liked, and weird facts Freddy would tell her, mostly about animals: *Did you know snakes smell with their tongues?* Stuff like that. But the notebook she pulled out that day was blank but for a small title Freddy had written on the first page for her, in large, messy letters: *Notes from New York.* Monica started writing, not song lyrics, but details about barrels, and flexibility, positions on the stage, and dance moves. Anything Maria yelled out, Monica wrote down.

The routine was more physical and complicated than anything Monica was used to. Worse, rehearsing onstage meant not having a mirror. A mirror was every performer's best friend. Monica got a lump in her throat just watching them. She could tell the kids had practiced this scene before. Maybe a few times, or maybe for a few weeks? She didn't know. But she did know she had a lot of catching up to do. And quickly.

"No, no, Hudson! Find your center of balance." Maria stopped them again. "When you step forward, Hudson, it cues the crew to drop the ropes behind you. *Then* you roll. Please try to remember!" Hudson's face glowed red.

"Cue the roll. . . ."

They went over that roll a dozen times, and Hudson was still off by a beat.

"Hudson!" Maria stopped the music and jumped in his spot. "If you move too slowly, everyone is having to adjust, and then everything is off."

Finally, after a dozen more times, Hudson got it right.

"Remember, this scene is the dramatic climax. Good guys meet bad guys. High energy. The audience must feel the intensity. It is your job to make them feel the intensity. Every line, every single move must be *perfect*. Every cross-over, every sequence, every jump and stomp exactly in time with the music. Are you listening? Monica from California, write this down: No missteps."

Monica wrote it down.

"One misstep can ruin the entire scene. No missteps!"

Maria's eyes trained on Hudson.

"Bad reviews are the kiss of death in this industry. And I don't attach my name to bad reviews."

The kid actors looked at one another nervously.

Maria inhaled. Hugh inhaled. The kids inhaled.

They all slowly exhaled together.

Monica took more notes.

After two hours spent on the same sequence, Maria finally said, "Well, okay. You're done." The kids cheered. "Go do a pizza lunch or watch cute videos online or whatever you kids like to do to celebrate the end of a hard rehearsal," she said.

The kids were just hopping off the stage when a loud *thud-thud-thud*, followed by a hollow scream, came from the side of the stage. The group turned to see a tipped-over barrel and Hugh Lavender writhing in pain at the bottom of the stage's side staircase. Blood was gushing from his nose. It looked broken.

"*No!* Not Hugh!" Artie yelled. He came racing down the aisle in a panic.

The four kids looked at one another in disbelief.

Interlude

"Mama"

Look, Ma, I finally made it
I'm first in line
I can see it in your eyes
The tears we've cried
Today I'll try harder
I'll be better than before
We dreamed the dream together
And I want to be the one you're always
rooting for

It was never easy being the youngest of
three
It was always my fault when my family
couldn't agree
"Be more like your brother," you'd say every
day

I just wanted your love
To tell me I was okay
So I had to break the rules

FEARLESS

There was nothing to lose
Spent my life running from the pain
You all had put me through

But this is my chance to make things right
To prove once and for all that my star shines
bright. . . .

Five

WHAT KEYS ARE FOR

After rehearsal the other three kid actors made plans to go out for dinner later that evening and left together. They had invited Monica, but she declined. She wasn't sure why; maybe it was because she felt like an outsider. Monica sat quietly in one of the auditorium seats, studying the cracked walls, the glistening chandelier, the ornate details in the molding that framed the stage. She was tempted to call home, but Freddy needed to rest, and probably so did her mother and father after a long night at the hospital. She wanted to call Marissa, but she would be in school. So she left the theater.

Fortunately, Monica's abuelita was standing outside

the Ethel Merman Theater with two warm corned beef sandwiches wrapped in white paper, and a side of pickles in a round plastic container that was leaking juice. Her abuelita had this sense of always knowing when to be there when Monica needed her. Monica figured it was just something abuelas were good at. Being there. It was about to pour, but her abuelita was too wrapped up in the magic of New York City to notice anything as common-place as clouds.

"Worth flying three thousand miles for!" Monica's abuelita said, raising the sandwiches above her like a tro-phy. Her fancy feathered derby hat had been replaced with a New York Mets baseball cap.

"Did you get your nails painted?" Monica's tone was gently curious.

"Big Apple red! I couldn't resist," her abuelita laughed.

Monica politely took a sandwich. She wasn't hungry.

"Tell me about your first rehearsal on Broadway!" her abuelita said licking her wrist of pickle juice. "Bet it was different from rehearsals back home. What were the other actors like?"

"Talented." Monica looked down at the pavement.

Monica didn't want to have to explain the Hugh Lavender incident. And she *really* didn't want to tell her abuelita that Maria hadn't even let her rehearse with the rest of the kids. She had sat out the entire time while Maria stood in her spot, at her barrel, sang her lines, and performed each move perfectly. "Are you taking notes, Monica from California?" she'd say on occasion. But mostly it seemed Maria had been focused on the other three. It made sense to Monica, but it wouldn't make sense to her abuelita.

"Did you meet Maria Marquez?"

"Yes," Monica said quietly.

Her abuelita said, "Eeee!" and did a little shimmy. "What's she like? Is she strict? Did she yell at you?"

"Abuelita . . . can we talk about this later?"

Her abuelita looked at Monica. They walked in silence for a few beats.

"How about I tell you about my day, then." Her abuelita smiled. Monica nodded. "Well, after I left you at the Ethel Merman, I hopped in a cab and dropped all our bags off at the hotel. Don't worry, I didn't check into the room. I want us to do that together. Then I went searching for the Stage Deli. It's famous, you know. *Old* Broadway." Monica's abuelita divided Broadway into two categories: old Broadway and new Broadway. Old Broadway was when none of the actors had mics and they could still belt out ballads to a packed house. Old Broadway was when people dressed up for the theater and when ticket prices were cheap. It was a slower pace, but still exciting. New Broadway was fast and bright and big entertainment.

"When I got to the Stage Deli, there was no deli. It's now a nail salon. But"—she waved her nails again—"this is America, Kita. When one door closes, another door opens. Plus, I had time to kill. Then a man selling baseball hats told me about another deli with even better corned beef sandwiches. So I bought a hat from him and walked twelve blocks."

"Twelve blocks? Aren't you tired, Abuelita?"

"I'll sleep when we're back in Reedley." Her abuelita laughed and kept talking. "New York! Broadway! Kita!"

Monica couldn't bear the thought of telling her abuelita that the Ethel Merman Theater was cursed. That it smelled like a swamp and was held together by duct tape and glue. It would break her heart. It was her abuelita who had helped get her here, who had driven her to every vocal lesson, audition, and rehearsal.

Whenever Monica was in a new production, she would enter her abuelita's kitchen to scraps of fabric and paper patterns. "I may not be the best seamstress, but I know what Broadway costumes are supposed to look like from the album covers," Abuelita would say. Monica was always the best-dressed character in every production. When her parents were working, or busy with Freddy, back and forth to doctor's appointments, Monica spent endless nights at her abuelita's house watching old movies and singing Broadway tunes. Each new script for each new show, Monica's abuelita would say, "Let's attack!" and get the highlighter out to note Monica's lines.

How was she going to tell her abuelita that her one and only chance on Broadway didn't stand a chance? That they'd spent their life savings and flown all this way for a flop that probably wouldn't last on Broadway for more than a week?

By the time they reached the hotel, the wind was gusting so hard, people were scampering into cafes and restaurants to wait it out. The famous Novelotel didn't look that famous or even much like a hotel from the outside. Wedged between two nondescript six-story brick buildings, it could be easily passed by. "What made this famous?" Monica heard herself asking her abuelita.

"It's a very old hotel."

"It's famous for being old?"

"I guess so. Oh, I just love the smell of old hotels," her abuelita said, with her hands to her chest, as they entered the dark, musty lobby. To Monica, famous old hotels smelled like Freddy's lizard tank. The walls were the color of leather, the ceiling a brilliant blue to replicate the sky. Everything about the snug space felt dated and heavy.

A toad of a woman was hunched over on a small, uncomfortable-looking stool behind the check-in counter. She seemed to be napping.

Startled by the pair's movement, she shot up with "You checking out?"

"No," Monica's abuelita said eagerly, "we're checking *in*. Garcia. G-A-R-C-I-A."

The woman typed lethargically on her computer.

"Just two of you?" Her voice was groggy and slow.

"Yes. I left our bags here earlier."

The woman stared at Monica's abuelita, trying to trigger a memory.

"Right." The woman pulled herself off the chair and got their bags from the back room.

"My granddaughter is starring in a Broadway musical," her abuelita said, lifting her bag.

"I'm just kind of an understudy," Monica said, meekly picking out a peppermint from a candy bowl on the counter.

The woman stared at Monica and with a yawn said, "Room 304," and handed Monica two sets of keys.

"I bet you've seen lots of stars come and go in here," her abuelita said with giddiness.

"Tons," the woman answered without expression.

Monica's abuelita made her way to the elevator and spotted a trash can along the way. She went over and pulled out a plastic container. "Perfect!" she said. At the same time, the woman behind the counter said, tapping her head, "Garcia, Garcia . . . hold on."

She turned around to the wall of mailboxes behind her. A few boxes had mail, but most were empty.

"You Monica?" the woman asked.

"Yes."

"This came for you," she said to Monica, and handed her a white envelope.

It had her name on it in blue cursive. The penmanship was sloppy, so it looked like it read *Monico Gargamella*. Inside the envelope was a key. No note, just a key.

That was strange, Monica thought. The key was smaller than a house key, and gold-colored, not steel. It looked old. A secret key, Monica thought, or maybe just a key to her dressing room at the theater. Either way, Monica had no idea what to do with it, and she didn't want her abuelita to ask too many questions, so she tucked it in her backpack and decided to think about it later. She had quite enough on her mind.

There were many things wrong with their hotel room. For starters, there was no bed, just a pullout couch that hit a small leaky sink when it opened. There was no TV, either. Or toilet paper. "It's gorgeous! Very New York," her abuelita said, raising a shoulder and trying to sound encouraging. Monica gave her a sideways glance.

"We'll make it our own." Monica's abuelita opened the plastic container she'd taken from the lobby's garbage can, gave it a quick rinse, and emptied her change into it. "Our very own Freddy jar." She smiled. They had one at home, too.

She handed Monica one of the pennies. "You'll do the honors?" Monica pulled over a chair and placed the penny above the frame of the hotel door, like her father had done at home. "Brings in the goodness," he would say.

A loud knock at the door startled Monica's abuelita. Monica hadn't considered until that point that maybe some of the foreignness of New York was a little scary for her abuelita, too. She might not like sleeping in a dingy hotel or being away from family either. Her abuelita's home was nice and comfortable. It was a small A-frame near the center of town. The neighborhood was quiet. The woman next door walked a cat on a leash and brought over fresh-baked bread.

The house had a screened-in porch that sagged. Monica spent hours on that porch sipping lemonade and playing cards or reading books. Monica loved to read. A block from her abuelita's house was a corner store that sold penny candy. Monica would do odds and ends for her abuelita to earn enough money to buy saltwater taffy—a taste of the ocean. Reedley was in California, but it was a few hours' drive from the nearest beach.

Monica bet a part of her abuelita missed her cozy home.

A housekeeper was outside the hotel room with a handful of fresh towels and a few rolls of toilet paper. Monica's abuelita spoke to her first in Spanish, then in English, then in some sort of Spanglish. The woman responded the same way. She explained where the trash chute was located and what floor the closest ice maker was on. As the housekeeper was leaving, her abuelita asked if she could borrow a broom. The housekeeper gave her an odd look but went to look for one.

The woman returned with a broom and handed Monica's abuelita two clean drinking glasses. The woman expressed no sense of urgency for the return of the broom. She smiled at Monica and, looking at the drinking glasses, said, "The water in New York is very delicious. They call it the champagne of drinking water. It is true. They say it's why New York's pizza crust tastes so good. Fantástico."

Monica's abuelita swept the floors, then went around the room and flicked cologne onto the pillows and the table, and into each corner. After they figured out how to make the couch into a bed, which took a lot longer than it needed to, Monica's abuelita sat on a bumpy cushion of the bed and said a silent prayer, then massaged her arms and stretched her lower back. "Ay, heavy luggage on an old woman's body."

There was one positive feature of the room. It had a fire escape. A good one. One that Monica could sit on to listen to the sounds of the city without being seen. The hotel was a couple doors down from the Ed Sullivan Theater, where late-night shows were recorded. Funny, Monica had always assumed the late-night shows were live, not recorded in the early evening. Before unpacking her clothes, Monica sat out on the fire escape, which looked at nothing but the bricks of the neighboring building, and listened to the sound of laughter and clapping coming from below as they recorded *The Late Show*. The band would play short tunes to signal the ends of segments. Then there would be more laughter.

The sun was setting on Broadway, and the lights of the city were intensifying. If she'd been in California, she would just be getting out of school. She would be hanging out with Marissa or, if Marissa had Math Club, Monica would read until her abuelita showed up in her yellow 1965 Malibu convertible, which Monica's father had kept running for a lifetime.

Her abuelita called to her, "Kita, do you want to go out? I'm going to try to find that used bookstore we read about."

"No, that's okay. You can go without me. I need to unpack," Monica said, climbing in through the window. She blinked as her eyes adjusted to the darkness.

"Fresh air feels nice," Monica's abuelita noted as Monica slid inside. Monica nodded. But it wasn't like the wind that swept down from the California mountains, awoke the crickets, and rustled through the leaves of the one large elm tree and into Monica's bedroom at night.

After her abuelita left, Monica opened her suitcase and lifted out her clothes—they still smelled of home. She paused when she saw a pair of raggedy jean shorts tucked in the corner. She didn't remember packing them. Freddy must have shoved them in when she wasn't looking. She had worn those shorts the day before she left, when Monica and Freddy had climbed the wall of the middle school cafeteria and sat on the roof and made a pact that by the time she returned to California, she would be a famous Broadway star and he would be an astronaut. The cafeteria was U-shaped, which made the corners of the building easy to climb up. Anything and nothing were possible up there. "Anything" meaning their imaginations could go anywhere, and "nothing" meaning that going to the places they wanted to go, doing the things they wanted to do, seemed like a long shot in reality.

Inside one of the pockets of the jean shorts, Freddy had

tucked her lucky elephant necklace. She hugged it as a tear rolled down her cheek. Her father had given her the necklace many years ago. An elephant because it was one of the strongest creatures on the planet, yet one of the kindest.

Monica called home. Her brother answered right away. "Tell me about the rats! Are they everywhere? And are they really as big as bicycles?"

"Sorry to disappoint you, but I haven't seen one rat yet. Not even in the subway station."

"Aw, darn," Freddy said.

"Thank you for sending my lucky elephant charm."

"I didn't want you to forget it," he said. Then he yawned.

"Rough night last night, eh?" Monica said, trying to sound casual.

"They plugged me into the Machine."

"Blech. You hate the Machine."

"Yeah, but I like missing school."

"How are you feeling?"

"Meh." He paused, then said, "Have you met anyone famous?"

"No one you would know."

He breathed a few times through his mouth.

"Is it two hours ahead there?" he asked.

"Three."

"So is it dark out?"

"Getting there. But I don't think New York City gets dark the way Reedley does."

"So you won't be able to sing me to sleep."

"No. I'll probably be in bed by then." Sadness broke over her like a wave.

"Can you sing to me now?"

"Sure!" She closed her eyes and pictured him sitting up in bed in his plaid pajamas, with his lizard on his lap.

"You want to take the Spanish or the English?" Monica asked.

"Spanish."

"Okay."

Monica made up a simple lullaby tune and began to sing softly:

"I am always with you to sing along."

Freddy repeated the line in Spanish:

"Siempre estoy contigo para cantar."

"To hold your hand and sing out strong."

"Para tomar tu mana y cantar fuerte."

"Our song is the one that we share."

"Nuestra canción es una que compartimos."

"They try to stop us but we don't care."

"Intentan detenernos pero no nos importa."

She repeated the song two more times.

"That's enough for tonight. Promise me you won't sleep with the lights on."

"I like sleeping with the lights on," he said. "Darkness is overrated."

After they hung up, Monica looked at a text from Marissa that had come in during the call. It was a photo of Marissa doing a duck face.

Monica typed: Hi! It's been a crazy day. Had an actual practice on actual Broadway! She attached a photo she had taken earlier in the day of the actors rehearsing the barrel scene.

No way! Marissa responded right away. Followed by Is that HUGH LAVENDER?!?!

How did everyone but Monica know who Hugh Lavender was? She couldn't bear to say that that *was* Hugh Lavender before his nose got busted, so she just responded yes.

Are you filling up your notebook with song ideas?

Filling my notebook . . . but not with lyrics, Monica typed.

After a few beats Marissa responded. You okay?

Just tired. Sorry. Talk tomorrow?

Marissa sent back, Miss you, Mo! So proud!

Monica dropped the phone onto the sofa bed, then pulled out the mystery key and studied it. She went through all the possibilities. Maybe it was just a key to her dressing room, which would make the most sense. Or a key to something here in her hotel. Maybe her abuelita had slipped it to the woman at the front desk when she dropped off the luggage. But why? And what if she found what it opened, like a secret room or a scary dark closet, and she would need to step inside?

Maybe it wasn't a key to open something but a key to keep something out. A shiver took over her body. She slid the key onto her elephant necklace and clasped it around her neck, then tucked it away under her shirt. The hotel room took on a darkness that made everything look plum-colored. She wanted her abuelita to return.

Twenty minutes later, the door opened and her abuelita walked in, carrying a large ficus with little sparkling lights strung on every branch.

"I had no idea the blocks were so long here," she said, huffing. Monica scrambled over to help her. "Eight blocks is double what you think it's going to be. Look, the lights are battery-powered. Homey, isn't it?"

They set the houseplant in the corner of the room.

"Abuelita," Monica said, studying the plant and its twinkling lights. "I'm nervous."

"What are you nervous about?"

"I don't know, maybe forgetting my lines." Monica touched one of the leaves. It felt smooth and oily. She plopped back down on the sofa bed.

"No, that's not what you're nervous about."

Monica thought harder. "I guess I'm nervous about being an understudy in a lead role on Broadway." In Monica's mind, she was still just a Broadway-actor-in-training. A lead was, well, someone who could put posters up of their past shows all over their dressing room walls. Monica groaned and pulled the pillow over her face. She had found herself in an unimaginable situation.

"Oh, Kita, let out the reins."

Monica pulled her head back out from under the pillow and laughed. "Let out the reins" was an expression Monica's first voice teacher, Ms. Robbins, had always said. "Close your eyes, streeetch your larynx . . . now let out the reins!"

Her abuelita sat next to her on the bed. "The world has been looking for you."

Monica laughed. "No it hasn't. The world doesn't know I exist."

Her abuelita grabbed the pillow. "Don't hide from it. Now, right now, is Broadway's time to have you. Let it have you!"

Monica thought about this.

"Do you remember what your bisabuela would say whenever someone said they were nervous about something?" her abuelita asked. Monica didn't remember. Her bisabuela had died five years ago, which felt like a very long time. "She would say, ¡Ponte a trabajar!"

That night, Monica stayed up late, quietly studying her notes and learning all the moves of that afternoon's routine—the ducks, narrow escapes, parries, lifts, lunges, and turns—while her abuelita snored softly nearby. Finally, at two a.m., she turned off the light.

Six

AMANDA

Twenty-three days until opening night

It wasn't the best idea to eat a bagel in the pouring rain, but New York City bagels were a food group unto themselves, and Monica couldn't wait to try one. She stood under the awning of the bagel shop, savoring each bite, thinking what a miracle it was that her abuelita had let her walk to the theater on her own. The rain came at her sideways.

The city took on a whole different personality in the rain. Crowds thinned out; streets were quieter. Cars passing by made the sound of waves rolling onto shore. All the smells of the city were stronger when they got wet, too. People smells, dog smells, trash smells, food smells.

By the time Monica made it to the theater, she was dripping wet. The only thing that survived the four-block walk were her dance slippers, which she had double-bagged and tucked inside her rain jacket.

The street scene in front of the Ethel Merman was very different from the day before. Two large semitrucks idled out front, traffic moving slowly around them, without much ado. A dozen or more stagehands hurriedly carried large prop parts into the theater. Every part was labeled. One stagehand called to another, "Left living room wall. Act one." Another stagehand echoed, "Act one." Another stood by with a clipboard, checking off inventory.

A text came in from her mother that said, **Good luck today, my little star! You got this! Call when you can.** It was four thirty a.m. in California. Her mom would be up that early preparing breakfast and lunch for Freddy before getting a ride to the farm with some other women. Then her parents would drive to the farm in her dad's SUV, coffee in one hand, oldies playing on the radio. They would have already listened to the weather report at home. Monica smiled and texted back: **Hope you have good weather today. I'll call during break.**

Little did she realize, there were not many breaks on Broadway.

"Welcome to Oz," the stage-door doorman said in a thick New York accent, "home of the oldest working pipe organ and longest-running curse on Broadway." There was a beauty to this man that Monica could appreciate. He appeared tired, yet lively. *Old Broadway.*

"Heard I missed all the excitement yesterday. You must be the new new Tabitha. I'm Jimmy Onions, stage-door doorman and amateur magician. Wouldn't you know it, I had to get a crown repaired." He opened his mouth and pointed to the new crown on his tooth.

"Do these things happen a lot?" Monica asked.

"Yeah, I'm always gettin' my teeth fixed."

"No I mean the accidents in the theater."

Jimmy scrubbed the inside of his mouth with his pinkie finger and thought about it.

"Kid, I've been working this stage door long enough to have let in a president of the United States, two panicked art thieves, a sleepwalking tourist, and an opossum. You work someplace long enough, you see lots of things."

He took a hankie and dabbed the corners of his mouth and continued. "So I guess it depends on where you come from and the way you think about things." He set down the hankie and thought. "Is the Ethel Merman jinxed? Maybe. Maybe not."

Monica crinkled her nose.

"But I'll tell ya somethin', kid—never in my forty years workin' the door have there been two falls in one day.

Now, that's a new one!" Jimmy Onions opened the door to the backstage with a big laugh into the wall of darkness. The theater inhaled her.

"Monica." She heard a whisper in the dark. It made the hairs on her arms stand up. Again she heard her name. "Monica!" Then someone grabbed her. Monica let out a scream. April whirled out of nowhere. She was wrapped in a shawl.

"I've figured it out." April pulled Monica by the arm as if they had been best friends for years. "The curse of the Ethel Merman." They walked on swiftly. "I knew this place wasn't normal the moment I walked in. I mean, what is normal these days? But this is different, like the place has been forgotten or ignored or something"—then she paused—"or like there's a spirit presence or something watching us. Plus it's always cold. Like weirdly cold." They both went suddenly cross-eyed as they focused on their breath, which could be seen as they exhaled.

"Hang your stuff in there." April pointed to a small coatroom. Most of the hooks already had wet raincoats on them. Monica was careful not to let her wet things drip everywhere as she hung them up. She sat on the bench and removed her wet shoes, replacing them with her warm, dry dance slippers.

April led Monica out of the coatroom and down a narrow

hallway, their straight path interrupted by stage crew whisking by with walkie-talkies, a man carrying a saxophone, a group of actors leaning against the wall drinking coffee and talking, singers warming up their voices, and a good deal of hammering.

"So here's what I think," April said, walking around a dancer doing a plié. "I think the Ethel Merman's curse is to take away people's superpowers." She stopped and looked sideways at Monica. "Bear with me." They kept walking.

"We all have our own superpower. Mine is acting. I mean, I'm not trying to brag. Of all the things, that's just what I'm best at. So look at the facts: Hugh's superpower was his looks—that perfect nose of his, broken. And Tabitha. Her superpower was singing, and she couldn't hit a high note here to save her." April pulled on Monica's arm again.

They stopped in front of Chris's wig room.

"I hope you like your straight red hair that you'll be wearing in the show," April said.

Monica touched her thick curly brown hair, which was a bit frizzy from the humidity post-rainstorm.

"Okay, fine, maybe not red. I guess it's more of a dark auburn. I know most actors don't like wearing wigs—they're hot and itchy—but not me. The minute I put mine on, it's like goodbye, April; hello, insert-whatever-character-I'm-playing. Which camp are you in, yes wig or no wig?"

"I've never worn a wig in a production before," Monica admitted.

April's eyes got wide.

"Oh you are going to love it! I just know you're a wig girl."

They turned in to a small room, where a man was trimming a short-haired wig with precision. Two large mirrors over two dressing tables were cracked in several places and held together with duct tape. The room had an odd smell, like burned plastic.

"Is that Hudson's?" April asked Chris.

Chris had a comb clenched between his teeth as he focused on getting the bangs just right. He looked at April and winked, implying it was her wig.

"Mine!" she said. "I knew Artie would give Froggie short hair—I just knew it! Froggie should have short hair. I mean can you imagine someone like Froggie being worried about brushing out her long, gorgeous locks? She'd be too busy thinking about important things to think about."

Next to April's wig stand Monica spotted a beautiful, long, straight-haired auburn wig. She grinned, imagining herself in full character.

"Monica is the new Tony," April explained to Chris, who still didn't look up from his trimming. "She's replacing Tabitha."

Chris slowly turned with the comb still between his

teeth and studied Monica. Gently he put down his scissors and removed the comb from his teeth.

"Oh no, that won't do," he said, calmly shaking his head. "No, that won't do at all," he repeated, touching the auburn wig with admiration.

The girls looked at each other.

"Yes," April replied. "Monica is the understudy to the understudy of Tabitha. Or *was*. Now she's the lead."

"We'll go without a wig for you. Your hair already is giving me a 1980s feel. I just need to tease it out a bit more in the front to create the 'claw.' That was the style of bangs in the '80s. Grrrrowwwl!"

"Monica wouldn't mind trying it on, I'm sure," April said.

"Does Monica speak for herself?" Chris said, then put the comb back in his mouth and went back to precision cutting.

Monica stayed silent.

Hudson and Relly strolled in the room, filling up the tiny space completely. "Can we try on our wigs too?" Relly said.

"Whoa, check it out!" Hudson's wig was a full, frizzy head of brown locks.

"Is that mine?" Relly pointed to a straight, dark wig with a little bit of a swoop to the side. He slapped his knee, laughing. "I like that it feels Pax, but updated," he said.

"I thought you'd like it." Chris nodded with a sense of pride.

Monica tried to figure out why she was immediately upset about not getting a wig like the other kids. It was no big deal—it was just a silly wig.

On their way to their dressing room, April picked up a roll of duct tape and turned to Monica. "And anyway," April continued, "how does a glamorous Broadway theater go from having over a dozen Tony-winning productions to this?" They dodged a large piece of plaster crumbling off the wall.

"I was wondering that too," Monica admitted.

"We all have been. Me, Hudson, and Relly. Tabitha too."

Monica prickled at the sound of Tabitha's name.

They walked past a room where set designers were busy creating the pyrotechnic pirate ship.

"It's amazing, isn't it? Like Christmas!" April held her chest.

Several doors down was Hugh Lavender's dressing room. It had been emptied out. They both shivered.

"He's not coming back. I heard him telling Artie yesterday," April said.

Monica nodded firmly. She wasn't sure why she nodded. She did it in a way that said she agreed with his decision to leave. She didn't. His nose would have healed before opening night. He was being a baby about it was what she really thought.

"Bet this place gave him the creeps," Monica said, backing up her nod anyway.

"Yep. I don't blame him. Every single day since we started rehearsing, something bad, like unlucky bad, has happened." April stretched her shawl so that it wrapped around Monica. "It's got to be ten degrees colder in here than it is outside."

"Like what bad things?" Monica shivered.

"Trust me, you don't want to know."

Monica did want to know.

April went on to explain that stagehands didn't seem to even notice. Artie was oblivious. He'd get really upset for a few minutes when something weird happened, then keep going. Chris went on shaping wigs. Jimmy opened the stage door and did his magic tricks.

"You know in all those TV shows where all this bad stuff is happening to the kids and you scream at the TV, 'Where are the *parents*?' It's like that," April said.

They had arrived at their dressing room. April pulled out a piece of paper.

"I carry around this list." April gave the list to Monica.

Monica read the title: *Broadway Traditions*.

"Broadway actors are a superstitious bunch." April said.

Some traditions looked familiar to Monica. Of the dozen items, most had check marks next to them.

April leaned in and read aloud. "'Don't wear blue onstage. No peacock feathers or mirrors onstage either. Never say *good luck*, always *break a leg*. And—'"

"I still don't get that one," Monica interrupted.

"The leg isn't a body leg," April explained. "The leg is the curtain that hides the backstage. When an actor crosses the backstage to the front of the stage, where the spotlight is, they've broken past the leg to where they can be seen. All actors want to break past the leg and be in the spotlight."

"Right," Monica said.

April continued reading the list: "'It's good luck to give the director flowers stolen from a graveyard.'" She stopped. "We're not going to do that. We decided that wasn't really cool." April paused. "And also scary."

Two important must-dos on the list were lighting the ghost light at night, and performing the Legacy Robe ceremony on opening night, then afterward blessing the theater.

Monica remembered seeing ghost lights set up at her community theaters back home, but she hadn't thought of it as being a tradition.

"Theaters place a stand with a single lightbulb at the edge of the stage and light it every night after each performance. It must stay lit the entire night to ward off bad luck until performers return the next day," April said.

"Do you believe in that?" Monica asked.

"Of course! Don't you?"

Monica nodded.

"And then there's the Legacy Robe ceremony. It's one tradition all Broadway productions participate in with every new show. Everyone involved in the performance, actors and crew, stands in a circle the day of opening night, and one of the actors has the honor of wearing a robe with the name of the production stitched on it. I really really want to be the recipient of the robe for this show." April gave herself a big hug.

The stage manager ran up to them in a panic.

"Artie wants all of you onstage right away!"

The girls gave each other a look of concern. What was going on now?

"Well that didn't take the papers long." Artie stormed onstage, waving his phone around. *Broadway Times* had a large photograph of Hugh Lavender and his broken nose at the top of the landing page. The headline read: TELEVISION STAR INJURED AT THE ETHEL MERMAN AS MORE ACTORS LEAVE ABRUPTLY. The article continued: "'Is Hoffman's production losing steam before it even opens?'" Artie muttered as he read the words out loud. "'Is this little cursed theater too much for Hoffman?' *Too much for Hoffman?* I'll show them too much. Kids. Now!" He pointed to the floor. Relly and Hudson were already sitting right there. Monica and April scrambled to sit down next to them. Artie smoothed back his wild hair.

"Okay, you're all here. Good." He looked perplexed and pleased at the same time. "After a call from some of your parents yesterday"—Artie turned a hard stare on April, mumbled "and the union," and then went on—"I'm making some changes around here."

The four kids looked at each other nervously.

"Kids, meet Amanda St. Clair." He pointed to the curtain. A rustling of what sounded like a flock of birds occurred backstage, then nothing. Then, all of a sudden, out from behind the curtain came a woman whirling in a green-and-white polka-dot dress, holding a hot dog in one hand. She flounced over to the center of the stage and gave a big wave to the kids with her free hand, an enormous grin on her face.

Amanda St. Clair was a child tutor employed by Child Star Educational Services. Most long-running productions hired tutors to keep the child actors up on their studies, but Artie had never thought to do it for this one until the call came from April's mother complaining about the lack of supervision she'd heard about from April. Tabitha's understudy's tragedy was the final straw.

"After what happened, my mom called Artie," April said. "I could hear her yelling, 'Rehearsals only started a few weeks ago, and already you have one child running out of the theater screaming late at night, another child who almost breaks her neck a few days later, and then Hugh Lavender? Anything else happens and I'm pulling April from the production!' And my mom said Artie got real quiet. She could tell he was stressed! Then she asked who was watching us. And I guess that's why Amanda is here."

Monica just nodded.

"I got so turned around back there," Amanda said, collecting herself, her voice that of a songbird. "I walked into the broom closet thinking it was the entrance to the backstage," she said with a sensational laugh.

Artie shook his head. "Amanda, may I introduce you to . . ." He paused to consider how best to address the group sitting on the floor in front of him. "The squad," he concluded. "They're all yours."

With that he stormed off the same way he'd entered, grumbling something more about bad press.

"Hellooooo, squad!" Amanda's voice was playful. She initially gave off the impression of being scatterbrained.

"I know there's a lot of work to be done for the show." She followed that with a great exhale. "I'll lay it out for you, if Artie hasn't already. Has he already?"

He had not.

"Well, then." She paced the stage. "School lessons will begin every morning at eight thirty. Rehearsal starts at ten a.m. sharp and usually ends around six p.m. . . . maybe eight p.m. I heard you're a little behind schedule. One break for lunch, one break for snack."

"*One* snack break?" Hudson said in a quiet aside to Relly.

"One break." Scatterbrained she was not. "Since all of you are in most of the scenes, you will mostly be rehearsing on the stage. Sometimes you'll split up as you work through the scenes piece by piece. Monica, April, you both have solos; Relly and Hudson, a duet. So the stage manager will probably rotate you through two rooms— one for blocking scenes, one for the music director working on your solos and duets—and the stage will be for dance, since Artie has you using so many props and flying things and climbing ladders . . . and that waterfall scene! Goodness me! Fortunately you're young. My knees are crying just thinking of all that bending. Final week will be tech rehearsal, then the show has several days of previews for critics. Phew. Got that?"

Amanda was a pro. The kids looked at her in awe.

"Don't worry, you'll learn how to balance rehearsals and schoolwork, too. I'll teach you techniques. But first, on to the tour. I'd like to show you around."

"Tour?" April bristled. "We've been working in this theater for a few weeks already. The last thing we need is a tour."

"Well then, let's call it a dissection. I must teach you about the bones of this glorious creature! At the end of the tour—dissection—I'll show you a very special place. How does that sound?"

April looked resigned. It was happening anyway.

"'Special place'?" Relly asked, a little confused.

"Yes! Oh, it's just lovely," Amanda said.

The lights in the theater started to flicker. The kid actors looked around. Amanda kept talking as if she hadn't noticed.

Amanda led them away from the stage toward the box office.

"Welcome to what is called 'the front of the house.'"

April looked visibly annoyed. She already knew what the front of the house was.

"Do any of you know about the history of this theater?" Amanda asked.

"I know it's creepy," said Hudson matter-of-factly.

"Okay!" she said, keeping it positive. "This theater is magical. *Magical!*"

"Amanda, I don't mean to be obnoxious, but could this be a quick tour? We are really behind schedule, and Monica hasn't even had a chance to learn the routines or work on vocals," April said.

"And the show starts in less than a month!" Relly said.

Amanda agreed to speed things up. For the next thirty minutes, she entertained the kids with stories of Broadway old and new. Even April had to admit Amanda knew a lot.

The main staircase leading to the balcony seating was at the rear of the theater. At the top of the stairs, patrons were greeted by a life-sized gold statue of Ethel Merman herself in a frozen performance pose.

"Greetings, Ethel!" Amanda said. "Did you know Ethel Merman could sing a high C for sixteen bars without straining her voice?"

"Wooow," said the kids.

On the pedestal of the statue was a plaque with the dates of Ethel's birth and death and, in matching gold lettering:

> Be yourself; it's the one thing you
> can do better than anyone else.
> —Ethel Merman

They all read the quote silently. Amanda nodded, saying nothing. A small smile appeared on her face. She looked at the kids for several seconds that seemed kind of awkward. Finally, she unwrapped the hot dog and took a bite.

"I've always wanted to take in the beauty of this place close up," Amanda said between chews, leaning against Ethel as if they were best friends having a chat. Her youthfulness masked her actual age; she'd been tutoring for almost twenty years.

"You know," she said, deepening her stare toward Ethel as if she were speaking directly to the golden actor, "this is the first time I've really experienced the Ethel Merman."

The foursome looked at one another. "Kind of seems like you took your first steps in this theater," Hudson said.

"Oh, well thank you! I like to think I know a lot about these old Broadway theaters." His comment made Amanda glow with happiness.

"How do you know so much?" April was genuinely curious.

"Well now, I've taken tours—of more than a few of these theaters, I assure you—and I've lived a long time. Ha! Time will give you knowledge in strange ways." She looked at the kids, who stared back blankly. "Let's see . . . I go to the

Performing Arts Library a lot and get magnificently lost . . . and I tutor. Your squad, as you call yourselves, is the first I've tutored here. Come to think of it, not many child actors at the Ethel Merman. Not many at all."

Amanda took another large bite of the hot dog. "I'm so sorry. I know this is rude. I haven't eaten anything all day." It was still early morning. She thought for a moment. "Time blurs when you're on Broadway. Long rehearsals and lack of sunlight will do that to you. You'll see." She winked as if letting them in on a big secret. The kids couldn't help but notice a large glob of ketchup caught in the corner of Amanda's mouth. They already liked her very much.

After a whirlwind trip around the main auditorium, she brought them backstage to show them how certain rooms in a theater functioned. April was again visibly annoyed. "We know where the wig room is. . . .We know what backstage looks like. . . . Yes, the sound room." She yawned. Relly had his notebook out. He'd only been in one production on Broadway, and only because his dance teacher had gotten a small part in a musical, and he got an even smaller part as her son. Hudson peppered her with other types of questions: "Does this place give you the creeps? How often do actors actually break a leg, in your opinion?" Monica felt too new to do anything but observe. What she observed was that Broadway attracted big personalities.

"This is a dressing room. . . ."

"I know where my dressing room is," April said in a monotone voice.

Amanda continued to lead them around all three floors of the building, through the theater's narrow hallways. Back on the first floor, she took a turn that at first didn't seem to lead anywhere. Then she opened a door. April perked up. She'd never been in that section of the theater before. "What is this?" she asked. The door led to a corridor of small rooms. The mood shifted entirely. Now they were secret agents. Most of the rooms' doors were closed. A few that were open had old props and wardrobes in them from past productions.

"This is the old part of the theater, when they used to have much larger productions." She stood for a moment and thought. "I suppose they don't have large productions here anymore. So no need to use the space." She bit into her hot dog. Relly took down notes.

"Why not?" asked Hudson.

"Large productions are expensive and, well, the Ethel Merman doesn't really draw those kinds of crowds anymore."

"I guess the old part of the theater also doesn't get heat," April said, shivering under her shawl.

"And now the fun part."

Amanda put her hand on a glass doorknob and said something under her breath. The kids leaned in to hear. She laughed a vibrant laugh. "You must think I'm weird. Sometimes I whisper a little saying to bring luck when I enter an important room." Monica smiled. She did little things like that too. With another laugh, Amanda opened the door. "Welcome to a very special place!"

The kids recoiled.

"Your new, very own classroom! Consider it your home away from home!" Amanda said with pride.

"This is disturbing," said Hudson.

A silence. Then Relly started to hum. Then sing. "Growin' up in the 'burbs . . ."

"They all think we're disturbed," April continued.

"We're never quiet and neat . . . ," Monica whispered.

They all began to sing quietly and perfectly in sync to the show's opening number, "Growin' Up in the 'Burbs."

> *Growin' up in the 'burbs*
> *They all think we're disturbed*
> *We're never quiet and neat*
> *Yeah, they all think that we're freaks*

We don't wear khakis like Dad
'Cause we're young and we're rad
With my friends till the end
On this little cul-de-sac
Adventure is always in store
'Cause we all want more

The makeshift classroom, far from the bustle of the auditorium, was dank and windowless. Compared to the energy and chaos of the rest of the theater, this was no-man's-land. Cut off from the rest of the world.

"I guess Mr. Hoffman really wants us out of the way," April said with annoyance.

"Cue the howling wolves." Relly imitated the sound of a wolf.

"Oh, bravo, Mr. Morton!" Amanda said. "You should get that recorded for the sound guys."

"There are no windows," Hudson said.

The old prop room had been cleared out and a classroom thrown together in its place just last night. The low lighting wasn't ideal for studying, and it smelled like wig powder and shoes. There was a long rectangular fold-up table in the middle, where all four kids would sit on the same side facing a dry-erase board, on which Amanda had written in cursive: *Welcome, April, Hudson, Monica, & Relly!!* Aside from a silly rubber chicken that hung by its waist from a blue rope on the wall, the room lacked any personality.

"Hey, I get it—chicken cord on blue!" Hudson laughed from the doorway.

"I don't get it," Relly said.

"Chicken cordon bleu. It's a chicken dish with cheese in the middle," Hudson answered with a full smile, dabbing lightly at the perspiration that had collected on his brow. Hudson wasn't a fan of narrow hallways or narrow rooms, but he was a fan of talking about food.

"Correct! Well done, Hudson, well done! Sometimes, kids, the answers are right in front of you! That's your first lesson of the day."

She went to the board and wrote under their names, in the exact same cursive, *Sometimes the answers are right in front of you.*

"Excellent work."

Then she pulled out a little sheet of gold-star stickers and placed one on Hudson's shirt. He blushed. "Uh, thanks," he said. The other kids laughed.

"Who else wants stickers?" Amanda said. They all raised their hands.

The silliness was shattered by plumbers clanking pipes in the boiler room below. "The waterfall saga continues," April said, shaking her head. The mechanics of the waterfall had been a problem for the stage crew all week. The Ethel Merman's old pipes could only manage to kick out a trickle of water a few pathetic pulses at a time down the tongue-shaped slide that was needed for one of the musical's pivotal scenes.

"Or the curse of the Ethel Merman," Relly said with a hint of excitement.

"Amanda, what do you know about the Ethel Merman's curse?" April asked bluntly.

"Hmm. I don't know about the theater actually being cursed—bad productions and some accidents here and there, sure, but otherwise, I just don't know. I suppose I think anything that seems unexplainable usually has an answer," Amanda said.

"What do you mean by that?" April quizzed her further.

"I mean, after all, the theater is a place where stories are told and released into the world and given life. Don't you think? Sometimes the messages cross and stir up the energy of a place."

"Stir up energy? Like ghosts?" April continued to probe.

"Hmm. I don't know about ghosts. Let's see." Amanda tapped her chin. "You know how when you're really little you think there are monsters under your bed?"

Hudson raised his hand. "Still do."

"It's just your imagination." Amanda smiled.

Could Amanda be right? Monica thought. Were all the things happening in the theater just monsters under their beds?

"You mustn't give those rumors of a curse too much importance, or they'll get you." With that she jabbed Hudson in the arm playfully with her finger. At that very moment, a loud crack of thunder rocked the building, and the lights in the classroom went out. Pitch-black.

Hudson was the first to scream.

April grabbed at the list of traditions in her pocket. Monica held on to her elephant necklace and whispered a little prayer in Spanish.

"Amanda, you there?" Relly whispered.

"I'm here," she said casually.

"What do you think about the curse of the Ethel Merman now?" Relly whispered in the dark.

"What do I think? Hmm. What do I think . . ." Amanda thought for a moment. "Well, I don't think losing power during a thunderstorm is related to any curse, if that's what you mean. Old theaters have old systems. There are answers for everything, my dear squad. Answers for everything. I'm sure the power will be back on any minute."

It didn't come back on, so they managed to feel their

way back to their dressing rooms with help from their cell phone flashlights and packed up for the day. Artie had called off rehearsals due to the power outage.

"Want to grab an early lunch with us? Great pizza parlor around the corner," April said to Monica as they felt around for their things.

Monica hesitated. She thought maybe she should be with her abuelita.

"Come on, one slice," April said. "Bet you haven't tried New York City pizza yet, have you?"

Monica smiled. "I hear the tap water gives it its yummy crust."

Joe's Pizza was bustling, even midmorning. Relly and Hudson were already sitting at the counter eating a pepperoni pizza. Hudson was in the middle of critiquing the sauce while Relly took a video. April pulled out her phone and took an action shot of the four of them. *#sliceoflife*

"So do you think the power going out is just bad luck or the curse?" Hudson asked between bites.

"Curse, definitely." April grabbed a piece of pizza and blew on it to cool it down.

"Hugh's nose?" Hudson went on.

"Oh man, total curse," Relly said, wiping his mouth and laughing.

"And just as we'd finally gotten the routine down," Hudson said.

"How long have you been rehearsing it?" Monica was curious.

They all thought for a moment.

"A week," Relly said.

"A week!" Monica was surprised. "How long have you been rehearsing for the show?"

"A little over a month," April said through bites.

This did not make Monica feel any better, and the group could sense it.

"Don't worry, we'll help you catch up," April reassured her.

"Yeah. It's not your fault you came in late," Relly said. "Artie called in a bunch of understudies kind of as emergency backup when he saw that things weren't going smoothly." Monica realized in that moment it was the reason she got the last-minute call to head to Broadway.

"I have a confession," Hudson said, finishing his root beer. "I've never seen anyone break their nose before, and when I saw all that blood . . . I thought I was going to faint." He shivered.

Monica was used to the sight of blood. She'd stopped counting the number of times Freddy would have a seizure and bang his face or bite his tongue.

"Hey!" Hudson said, changing the subject and the mood. "Anyone want to play Broadway Barnyard?"

Relly and April said yes. They looked at Monica.

"What's Broadway Barnyard?" Monica asked sheepishly.

"Someone starts out by singing a song in a farm-animal voice—you know, like clucking like a chicken or something to the tune of a Broadway song—and the others have to guess it," April explained. "I'll begin." April thought and thought, cleared her throat, and began: "Oink, oink, oiiiiiiink, oinky . . ."

"Helloooo, Dolly!" Hudson answered, singing the tune.

Hudson followed it up with a song from *Fiddler on the Roof* in cow. When it was Monica's turn, she did a song from *Starlight Express* in sheep. Her *baa-baa*s made Relly fall off his stool with laughter.

By the time they were finished, their bellies hurt from laughing. They even got some of the people in the pizza place to join in. A gruff guy making pizza behind the counter sang an Italian song in duck quacks. Monica had a new feeling about the production. Giddiness. Broadway kids were pretty cool. Now all she had to do was work extra hard to catch up. And keep up. Secretly, she worried she would never be as good as any of them. In fact, she worried about that quite a lot.

She was also worried about the actual show. Amanda was wrong. The power never came back that day or on Thursday or on Friday. They were losing valuable rehearsal time.

Interlude

"Growin' Up in the 'Burbs"

They say, "Kid, get in line
Do just what you're told"
But if I listen to them
I'll grow crabby and old
Instead I want to be seen
Shout out loud, and feel free
And when you hang out with a crew
That likes you for you
You'll never feel alone again

Growin' up in the 'burbs
They all think we're disturbed
We're never quiet and neat
Yeah, they think that we're all freaks
We don't wear khakis like Dad
'Cause we're young and we're rad
With my friends till the end
On this little cul-de-sac

Adventure is always what's in store
'Cause we all want more

It's our time
To show what we've got
Yes, it's our time
To be what they're not

Just a little bit braver
A little bit wiser
So don't hesitate
Before it's too late
'Cause today's all we know
So come on and let's go

I know it will be different
Today of all the days
'Cause the tires on these bikes
Won't lead us astray
We pedal faster than the guys in *E.T.*
And we're fighting for justice
For more than just me

It's like Duckie and Rocky when they had
enough
People thought they were losers
But they had the stuff

They just had to find it, way buried within
It's like us without prom and Adrian!!!

'Cause it's our time
To show what we've got
Yeah, it's our time
To be what they're not

Just a little bit braver
A little bit wiser
So don't hesitate
Before it's too late
'Cause today's all we know
So come on and let's go

Yeah, it's our time!

Seven

BREAK A LEG

Twenty days until opening night

Early Saturday in New York City, and the sun threw glorious reflections on every surface, creating a paradise of glass. Day five, and Monica's jet lag was finally gone. Seven in the morning felt like seven in the morning and nine at night felt like nine at night again. Because of the power outage, Maria had announced they would be reporting to the theater over the weekend to make up for the missed days of practice. Monica popped out of bed eager for rehearsal, her head filled with thoughts. "Confidence!" she told herself, looking in the mirror. And, pointing a finger: "And I mean it."

Though this would only be Monica's second time walking from her hotel to the Ethel Merman Theater, since they couldn't rehearse in the dark with no power, she knew her way easily. Playing hide-and-seek in the orange groves back home gave her a good sense of direction. Still, her abuelita had made sure to give her a list of landmarks to memorize. If Freddy were there, he'd be skipping next to her, counting something on the walk. Taxicabs or trash cans or trodden-flat pieces of chewing gum on the pavement. Freddy called them pavement freckles. There weren't a lot of sidewalks in Reedley, except for a few sections of their small downtown, so pavement freckles were a little more of a rare find than in New York City. When she walked to the Ethel Merman that perfect Saturday morning, she noticed freckles everywhere. She smiled. Far, far from home. She rubbed her elephant-charm necklace and noted her last landmark. It still felt like a big deal to be walking around New York City alone.

She wanted to call Marissa and tell her every detail of the city. Then she wanted to call Freddy and her parents and tell them every detail. But they would all be sleeping. The time difference and her rehearsal schedule would make calling home this weekend almost impossible.

Ahead, the Ethel Merman looked a thousand years old, but grand and strong in the bright sunlight. She didn't get it, the curse thing. Her father would have said, "Sometimes there's nothing to get."

Jimmy Onions answered the door before she even had a chance to press the buzzer. "I have an amazing sense of timing," he said with a welcoming smile, holding a bowl of cereal in one hand. "And a security camera," he chuckled.

"You work on Saturdays?" Monica asked.

"I was going to ask you the same question. Sometimes I work Saturdays." Then he clarified, "When weekend shifts don't show, I'm the first to get the call." He returned to his space inside. "So, weekend shift didn't show."

"Why not?"

"Eh, you know, kids these days. They don't wanna work the weekend shifts." He put his spoon in his mouth, pulled it out, and said, "No offense."

"Maybe the curse scared them away," Monica said, itching for a conversation that veered in that direction.

"I don't know nothin' about nothin'. Sometimes people are unreliable and they don't show up for their shifts, and then I gotta back out of my weekend poker game with the boys and here I am on a Saturday morning. Voilà-dee-da. That's all I know."

Monica noticed a *Playbill* for *Dreamgirls* sitting on one of his shelves. It was the first musical she had ever seen. She remembered the night vividly. It had been her sixth birthday, a balmy Tuesday in June. Like any other night, her parents were making dinner, and she was setting the table, when her abuelita walked through the front door all dressed up and laughing.

"Where are you going?" Monica asked.

"Not where are *you* going—where are *we* going!"

The show was at the community theater in the next town over. By all standards, it was a small theater, without the best acoustics or lighting, but as far as Monica was concerned, it was Broadway. The actors were amazing. That night changed Monica forever. She had been transported to a different world. Afterward her abuelita managed to get them backstage for autographs.

"Do the actors perform a lot?" Monica asked.

"Of course. Every night. It's their job." Her abuelita smiled.

Job? She wandered out of the theater, stunned and inspired. "I'm going to do what they just did. I'm going to do that for the rest of my life!"

Jimmy followed her eyes to the *Playbill* and asked, "You seen it?"

"Once, when I was really little." Her voice trailed off as she held the memory a bit longer before she snapped back to reality.

"Nothing like Motown to get the blood flowing." He closed his eyes and bobbed his head. "I've seen probably close to a thousand shows, and every single one was a blessing and a gift. Even the flops! Especially the flops."

He handed her the *Playbill*. "Here, take it, kid." It had been autographed by the cast members. "Been meaning to clear out some stuff in this place anyway."

Monica took the *Playbill*. "Thank you so much," she said.

"Want to see a magic trick?" he asked.

"Sure."

Jimmy showed her his hands. Nothing in them. Then he reached behind her ear and pulled out a shiny penny.

"Ta-da!"

He handed her the coin.

She studied it.

"Can you help me with something?" Monica asked. "It's kind of a strange request."

"Kid, this is Broadway. If it's not strange, we don't want it."

"Can I place this above the door?"

He looked at the penny. Looked back at her and gave her a hint of a smile. "Sure, kid. Just a sec." He picked up the stool and placed it under the door. It wobbled. He held it while she stood on her tiptoes. She had a flash of her brother helping her climb up onto the cafeteria's roof. Her parents lifting her up into the olive trees. She was here, now, at the top of something fantastic. With a sense of urgency, she placed the penny. It made a flat clink.

"Got it!" As she leaned to climb down, the mysterious key on its chain slipped from where it was tucked away in her shirt into full view. Jimmy's eyes went wide, and for an instant his face made an expression as if he were hallucinating. He hurriedly helped her down, and, looking straight into her eyes, he whispered, "Find it."

What? What did he mean by that?

She quickly tucked the key back into its hiding spot, and Jimmy Onions turned toward his stool as if no words had ever been exchanged. Had she imagined it?

To Monica's relief, the buzzer of the stage door sounded, breaking the moment. Jimmy opened the door to Hudson, who hustled in with wet hair and a Tupperware of baked goods, "Cronuts!" Hudson said in his usual grand voice. "Croissant-doughnuts!" he explained.

Onstage, Relly was curled up in a sleeping bag with headphones on, bobbing his head with an extra nod to Monica as she walked in.

"Did you sleep here?" Monica asked, studying Relly's sleeping bag.

"Huh?" He removed his headphones.

"Did you sleep here?" she repeated.

"My mom had an early-morning shift at the hotel. I came in with her. Theaters are great places to nap." Relly yawned. His mom worked two jobs. One was cleaning rooms at one of the largest hotels in all of Manhattan—1,966 rooms. Evenings she waitressed at a small diner near their apartment.

"Lunar eclipse last night. Did you see it?" Relly asked, sitting up. "Can't see stars when you live in the city, but you can see eclipses." Relly lived in a small, two-room basement apartment in Harlem with his brother and mother. On warm nights he would sneak up to the apartment building's rooftop garden. It was nothing more than a wooden platform with a few chipped urns, some abandoned raised planter boxes, and a couple of old trellises laced with dead vines. A few years earlier it had been a lush oasis. The garden had been tended his father. But then his father passed away. Now Relly headed up to the rooftop to talk to his father in the sky.

Hudson came in, announcing his Cronuts, with a few already taken off the platter, followed closely behind by April.

"Rush hour on a Saturday. I can't even!" April had the farthest commute of all of them. She, her three older brothers, her mother the schoolteacher, and her dad the dentist lived in a nice suburb in New Jersey about an hour outside the city. They all took turns driving her into the city. Monica wasn't really sure what town she actually lived in because April just referred to it as Planet Mars.

When they were all together, Relly said in hushed tones, "Did you hear what happened last night?"

None of them had heard anything.

"A security guard got scared away by the curse of the Ethel Merman in the middle of the night. He was seen running for his life down Forty-Fifth Street," Relly said, looking excited.

"How do you know that?" April asked.

"I overheard the stage crew. When they saw me, they stopped talking. Then, when I asked them if I had heard them right, they denied it and told me to go run my lines or something."

"That's weird," Hudson said.

"Yes. But it's a clue. Now we know something's going on. Not just monsters under our bed." He raised an eyebrow, glanced around the room. "So we investigate."

"How do we investigate?" asked Monica.

"*What* do we investigate?" emphasized April.

"We start by interviewing the security guard." Relly smiled and nodded.

Amanda breezed in, interrupting their scheme.

"Oh how glorious! The lights are on and everyone's back to dancing and singing today!" She smelled like clean laundry. Her auburn hair was perfectly set in big curls. "Mr. Fernando will be happy to see this," Amanda continued.

Her eyes widened as she saw Hudson's offering and took a Cronut. "Oh! Did you make these? Don't mind if I do," she laughed. She looked at the Cronut and started to sing to it in a quavery voice, lyrics from the *The King and I*:

> *Getting to know you, getting to know all*
> *about you*
> *Getting to like you, getting to hope you like*
> *me . . .*

And then she took a big bite.

April pulled out her phone and snapped a shot of her own Cronut. *#cro-whats?*

Hudson looked at Monica. "Theater people."

"Who's Mr. Fernando?" Monica asked April.

"Fernando Speldini, a.k.a. Mr. Fernando," April answered, holding the *aaah* to make his name *Fernaaaando*, "is our vocal coach. He took a break for a few days. We weren't sure if he was coming back." April gave Monica a sideways glance, like Monica should be figuring something out.

"He worked on *The Phantom of the Opera* and *Aladdin*," April said.

Monica raised her eyebrows to say she was impressed.

"Yes, I was in *Aladdin* with him. He's brilliant. You'll love him," April said.

"Twenty days until opening night, people!" Maria walked onstage and threw each of them a golf ball. "And in those twenty days, you will each learn this." She tossed one, then two, then three golf balls in the air above her head with one hand, and in perfect rotation caught each one in the other.

"Juggling?" Hudson's voice hit a pitch higher than usual. None of the kids knew how.

The "ballroom" number. The second scene of the musical, when the kids eavesdrop on a conversation the golf-course developer is having with a neighbor, and discover that it's the kids' houses that are set to be destroyed. The scene begins: "A bulldozer?" "A bulldozer!"

April took a quick phone shot of the group with golf balls in their hands. *#golfanyone?* She would wait awhile to post it. April had just under ten thousand Insta followers but planned to get her numbers up before opening night with some fun behind-the-scenes images. "People who post between two and ten images a day get the best results," she explained to Monica.

"This is where Mr. Morton's professional ballroom-dance experience will be beneficial," Maria said.

"I mean, I wouldn't call it professional," Relly said, looking at the golf ball as if it were moldy bread. "But I did rock a sequin jacket in a ballroom regional championship.

Pretty sweet," he added, smiling and nodding. That had been his dance teacher Miss Sandra's idea. She lived in the apartment above Relly's and had begun taking him to her dance studio after school to help out his mother, who needed childcare. One day Relly was goofing around in the mirror to music, and Miss Sandra immediately recognized that he had talent.

"You, my little Relly Button, are a natural dancer!" She was right. He trained with her for years, but never in any sort of dance-competition kind of way. Then her ballroom-dance partner broke his hip a week before a big tournament, and Relly was the only one who fit into his costume. As you can imagine, Miss Sandra's dance partner was a small man, but big in moves and personality. Relly and Miss Sandra went all the way to the championship that year. And won.

Maria grabbed a roll of blue painter's tape. "We're going to work on our blocking for this scene today." She stood there for several seconds, tapping her mouth and looking at the stage. The kids watched with curiosity as she marked off new areas. She began with the center line. "Center, here." The center was most important when actors sang their solos. Monica had learned that the hard way. When you didn't hit your center mark, you didn't hit the spotlight. When you didn't hit the spotlight, you sang in a shadow and no one could see you. It had happened her very first show. It never happened again.

"Hudson, can you do a backflip from a standing position?" All the kids looked at her with wide eyes. "Never mind, we'll skip that for now."

She took three large steps, pulled another piece of tape, ripped it with her teeth, and placed another mark. Then three equal steps to the other side of center. Everything was precise. The symmetry was critical. She looked at the stage floor, satisfied.

Mr. Fernando walked in. He was a short, stout man with a turned-out walk and a really long purple scarf. "Good morning, everyone!" he said in a friendly way.

Everyone welcomed him eagerly.

"Mind if I borrow one of your dancers, Maria?" Mr. Fernando studied the children, and his eyes landed on Monica. "Ah. You must be Ms. Monica!" Monica smiled. Mr. Fernando shook her hand cheerily with both his hands and gave her a little hug.

They walked down the hall to the rehearsal studio. He asked her what part of California she was from. He'd never heard of Reedley. "But I'm sure it's beautiful!"

They turned in to Studio B. It was a small room with a piano and a wall of mirrors. A petite woman with round glasses like her abuelita's waved from the piano bench.

"We're going to work on your eleven o'clock number," Mr. Fernando said, referring to the big, showstopping number that happened toward the end of the second act. Monica's character would be singing it. "You're nervous," he added.

She nodded.

"Don't be nervous. I saw your audition tape. You're good." He handed her the music, then indicated the woman on the piano bench. "This is Mrs. Bigsley. Mrs. Bigsley is Broadway's most illustrious piano player." She took a sip of coffee, and then the lesson began.

They did a few voice exercises to loosen Monica's throat and wake up her diaphragm. Things like "Ha ha ha ha ha ha" and "He he he he he" and "Ho ho ho ho ho ho ho" and "Aaaaaaaaahhhh" sloping downward.

Mr. Fernando explained things clearly and started sentences with "We're going to . . ." a lot, which Monica liked. "We're going to see if you can hit this note without cracking." And "We're going to try that scale again."

They started to go over her eleven o'clock number. Just the first few bars. Monica's throat felt tight, and her voice kept cracking. "I'm sorry," she would say, and then they'd start over.

No matter how many times Monica goofed up, he would laugh this funny little hee-hee and wave it off. "We're going to work on that." He had a severe scar across his chin that stretched as he sang. Sometimes it looked like a second smile. Monica thought he was the perfect person to have two smiles. If it had been on Maria's chin, she would just have looked like she was doubly angry.

As much as he made her feel comfortable, she was doing a terrible job. She wondered if the Ethel Merman had taken away her superpower.

"Monica, how do you usually feel when you're singing?" Mr. Fernando interrupted as Monica flatted another note. "Just in general."

Monica thought for a moment. Did he mean physically?

"Don't be afraid to answer with your true feelings," he continued.

Be present and enjoy, her abuelita would say.

"I guess I don't feel so much like an underdog."

"An underdog! Oh, my dear, hardly."

"I guess maybe I feel a little special when I'm singing," she said quietly.

"Good, good. That's a very good answer. That's the feeling of talent." He paused. "And how do you feel when you're singing here at the Ethel Merman, on Broadway?" He smiled.

She thought for a moment. "I feel a lot like an underdog."

"And it's presenting itself in your voice." He smiled again.

He walked toward Mrs. Bigsley at the piano. "When

you have a special talent, you must do something about it. Don't ignore that feeling of thinking it's special."

Mrs. Bigsley took another sip of coffee.

"What do you love most about singing?" he asked, looking at Mrs. Bigsley but speaking to Monica.

"When I sing, I can turn into anyone I want to be." For a split second, she had a visual of her dad watching Elvis on TV and listening to Elvis's records. Her father had a terrible voice, but when Elvis came on, the sky was the limit. She and her father would sing along, doing Elvis's signature leg shake. They *were* Elvis. She would sing Madonna. She would sing Bette Midler. Julie Andrews. Anyone she wanted to be in that moment. Any feeling she wanted to feel.

"Tony has two big solos. Your voice is the reason you got the part." Monica wanted to correct him. She didn't get the part—she got the part after two others got the part. She wondered if Mr. Fernando knew that. Of course he did. Then she wondered if *he* had left her the key. She was tempted to ask him about the curse, but instead she asked a question that she immediately wanted to take back: "Mr. Fernando, am I good enough?"

How embarrassing. Why had she asked him such a silly question?

Mr. Fernando looked at her. His warm smile turned

into a frown. "Never be good enough" was all he said. Mrs. Bigsley sipped her coffee.

When Monica returned to the stage an hour later, still having not quite sung very well, she expected to hear Maria yelling at the full cast. Instead she was standing center stage with a bag of golf balls around her wrist, writing notes in the margins of the script.

"Where'd everybody go?" Monica asked.

The cheeriness of earlier that morning had vanished.

"Your friend Hudson is missing."

"What do you mean, 'missing'?"

"Gone."

"He left the production?" Monica knew Hudson had been frustrated working with Maria. He would explain that his character wasn't meant to be graceful on his feet. But Monica had never imagined he would abandon the production entirely over it.

"Just gone." Then Maria explained. Relly had had no problem with the complicated dance moves, and April had managed as well, but Hudson was finding them impossible. *My body just doesn't move that way!* Hudson had complained. He slowed down the rehearsal. They took a long water break. Hudson was tired. "After break, everyone returned but Hudson." Maria shrugged. "If he doesn't return soon, we'll get his understudy out here."

She slapped the pen down on the script and looked straight at Monica.

"Sometimes these shows just don't work out."

She tucked the script under her arm and left. Monica sat down on the wing of the stage. Her eye caught sight of a golf ball in the orchestra pit. She heard and then saw Artie enter the theater from the rear. He was with a tall man in a gray business suit. Monica could make out their words very clearly, because the tall man had a very loud voice, and Artie had an even louder voice.

"I don't want to say it—I dread it, really—but this might be the end of the line for the Ethel Merman," Artie said with his arms crossed.

The man in the gray suit put a gentle hand on Artie's shoulder. "Hard choices, but I think you're making a wise decision, Artie."

"Truth is, Broadway musicals need to run a really long time just to break even." Artie took a long look at the theater's grandeur and sighed. "What did you say your vision is for the place?"

"A luxury hotel. Bigger and shinier than NYC has ever seen." The man in the gray suit corrected his posture so as not to appear too eager.

"Huh, don't we have enough hotels on Broadway?" Artie said with a furrowed brow.

"Not like this one! A place to look down on Broadway from the roof deck swimming pool!" The men's voices trailed off as they walked out the same way they came in.

Monica studied the golf ball.

Moments later, April, Relly, and Hudson returned to the stage, arguing.

"I wasn't *missing*; I was stuck in the bathroom!"

"You were gone for like thirty minutes."

"You think I don't know? The door was jammed. Didn't you hear me screaming?" Hudson was sweaty, furious, and embarrassed all at once.

"We thought the curse got you," April said.

"Can you imagine Artie when the headline reads 'Actor Goes Missing *Inside* the Ethel Merman'?" Relly slapped his knee, laughing.

"There are like a dozen bathrooms in this theater, and I get the one with the sticky lock!" Hudson said.

They noticed Monica and went over to her.

"And then my mind started imagining things."

He explained that when he was in the bathroom, he thought he'd felt the temperature drop and a presence of something. Then the lights had started to flicker. "Did the temperature *really* drop? Was there a presence? Did I imagine the lights? I don't know. I freaked out. When I tried to open the door, the lock broke and the door jammed shut. I stayed there a long time, not moving. Just hoping the presence would go away and the lights would stop flickering." Hudson sat down on the stage. He was growing pale. "This place is getting to me."

"How'd you get out, then?" April asked.

"I don't like small spaces. So finally I just freaked out and busted through the door."

"Cool!" Relly said, raising his fist in the air. Hudson rubbed his arm. Everyone noticed for the first time that his sleeve was torn and he was bleeding.

"And because of me, Maria left, and we'll be even further behind schedule."

He slid his *Our Time* script across the stage floor. "Let's just write the reviews ourselves: 'Artie Hoffman's Production Biggest Flop Ever on Broadway.'"

"One plus: When you went missing, I found the number for the security guard who was on duty last night," Relly said.

The kids perked up.

"Wanna call him?" Relly was already dialing the number.

April politely reached for the phone. She smiled. "I'm really good at talking to adults."

Relly gave her a sideways glance and handed the phone over.

The guard answered on the third ring. He was still rattled by the events of the night before.

"I'd never seen anything like it," he said. He was a soft-spoken guy. "Haven't been doing this job long, but some things just aren't right."

"What did you see!" yelled Hudson in the background.

"Shhhhh," the others said in unison.

"What did you see?" April asked with an air of authority.

"Last night, I was doing my normal rounds through the theater. That's part of the job. To make sure things are secure, you know? Well. As I was making my rounds on the second floor, I heard a noise."

"What kind of noise?" Relly said, leaning into the phone.

"What kind of noise?" April repeated.

"Like a scratching, or rustling," he said with a shiver in his voice. "A lot of scratching and rustling."

"Scratching and rustling?" April imagined a terrible image of a trapped person. "Where was it coming from?"

"Well, it was coming from one room, but the door was closed. And I'm not that familiar with the theater yet. I just only started working there, you know."

The kids nodded in anticipation.

"You know?" he repeated.

"Yes, yes, go on!" Hudson said, pulling the phone toward him.

"Sorry, your voice just got deeper. Am I talking to more than one of you?"

April cleared her throat. "No, no, I apologize for that."

The security guard continued, "So I thought it was maybe someone's dressing room, but I guess it was some sort of kitchen."

The kids looked at Hudson. A few days earlier he had transformed one of the empty dressing rooms into a kitchenette for a few episodes of a FoodTube show he was calling *Broadway Sizzlers*. It had become really popular with viewers. Artie thought it was great publicity.

"And . . ."

"And I opened the door and . . . no, no, I can't."

"What was it?"

"Rats, dozens of them, the size of cats!"

"Oh no . . ." Hudson hit his forehead.

"Worst part was, they didn't run away. They just looked up at me with these beady red eyes and then went back to eating."

"Eating? What were they eating?"

"Oh no," Hudson repeated.

"I dunno. Smelled like bacon."

"Oh no!" Hudson moaned. Three days ago, when Artie had called them to the stage for their emergency meeting about the front-page Hugh Lavender news, Hudson had been in the kitchenette he had created, showing his FoodTube followers how to crisp bacon using a waffle iron.

"I completely forgot about it, with the headline about Hugh getting hurt, then the meeting with Amanda, and the power going out. . . . I just left the plate of bacon there."

"For three days?" they asked in unison.

"So it was the rats that scared you away?" Relly asked into the phone.

"No, no. I mean yes, but no. It was all that creepy stuff the others were doing late at night. The rats were just the final straw."

The kids were puzzled.

"Well, good luck." And he hung up.

"Wait—what creepy stuff? Who are 'the others'?" April demanded into a phone that was already disconnected. "What creepy stuff? Who are 'the others'?" she repeated to the group.

Relly flipped to a fresh page in his notebook and made a list: "So far: waterfall saga, two lead actors and an understudy all injured, a security guard goes running for his life, possible haunting in a locked bathroom, power outage, rat infestation, and now creepy stuff 'the others' do at night. Okay, so we're fine!"

Interlude

"Superhero"

Never expect the unexpected

You'll always be let down

Remain calm and collected

When other people are around

Just pretend you knew what would happen in the

game all along

Even though, at times, it seems all wrong

That's just for you to know

And they'll never find out

That you're not that brave and you're full of doubt

There's a superhero

Just waiting to guide you

That voice inside

That sounds a lot like you

Trust in yourself and where it's telling you to go

The one who's been there the most

You're never alone

Out there on your own

FEARLESS

After I polish my moves

And I'm ready to go

If I fall once or twice, they'll never know

'Cause I laugh it off

They'll never see me cry

They just see me at the end

When I can fly

There's a superhero

Just waiting to guide you

That voice inside

That sounds a lot like you

Trust in yourself and where it's telling you to go

The one who's been there the most

You're never alone

Out there on your own

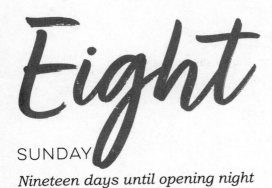

Eight

SUNDAY

Nineteen days until opening night

Miss Susan, the acting coach, walked into Studio A with beautiful long beaded cornrows, a flowing rainbow silk dress, and very straight posture. A grouping of gold bangles clinked together on one wrist as she moved. The four kids, who had been pink-eyed with sleepiness, suddenly perked up. "See how I just walked into the room?" Miss Susan said. "I took up space." A sense of liveliness breathed brilliance into the otherwise dreary rehearsal room.

"Today's Sunday," Miss Susan said, putting down her big, full purse. "I never work Sundays," she said in a cross tone. Then she smiled. "Why am I working on a Sunday?"

April raised her hand. "Because we need help?"

"Because you need help!" Miss Susan said with a laugh. "You've had a tough time so far," she continued. "But you're not gonna care about that. I'm not gonna care about that. You know what I'm gonna care about?" She turned and looked at herself in the full-length mirror, striking a dramatic pose. "Being buttery."

The kids laughed.

"What do I mean by that? I mean I'm going to be smooth with my body language, with my voice, with my presence onstage. My confidence. You won't be able to take your eyes off me."

It occurred to Monica that maybe they could talk frankly with Miss Susan about the problems at the Ethel Merman. Miss Susan swayed from side to side as she studied the kids. She didn't ask about Monica being new to the group. She didn't do small talk. She was very easygoing.

"Let's start with an improv exercise to warm up."

She pulled out a newspaper from her purse and, pointing to Relly and Hudson, said, "Why don't you two begin. One of you will sell this newspaper and the other will buy it. Act out the scene."

Relly took the newspaper and looked at Miss Susan. "I don't get it."

Realizing right away he had never taken an acting class before, she explained the exercise in greater detail.

"Imagine the setting. Create your characters. Buying a newspaper can be boring. Focus on drawing us in. Be careful not to overact. I'll give you ten seconds to talk about your approach, then a minute to act it out."

Relly and Hudson picked up on the exercise right away. Hudson would be the buyer, Relly the seller. In seconds they had the group laughing. A tug-of-war took place over the newspaper, and the boys flew through the air, chasing the paper and the money down the street. It was brilliant.

"Bravo!" Miss Susan applauded vigorously. "Perfect in-the-moment improv. Comedic timing, spot-on!"

Monica waited quietly, cross-legged on the floor, until Miss Susan's eyes landed on her. The truth was, Monica could get by on her acting skills, but she'd never in her life done an acting class, much less improv.

"Girls, your turn. Same scene."

April was already up and ready to tell Monica her idea for the scene. She had done these exercises a million times in acting class.

"Think about your props," Miss Susan said.

All they had for a prop was the newspaper, Monica thought. April whispered something to Monica and they giggled.

"We're ready." April said.

"Hello, ma'am. How much for the paper?" April said to Monica, with a twist in her voice and a goofy look on her face.

"It's your lucky day. Only twelve dollars for you!" Monica replied.

The others laughed.

Their bodies as props, they used their height difference as comic relief.

Monica passed the newspaper over April's head. April dramatically tried to jump and reach for the newspaper as Monica acted as if nothing was wrong. Then April went higher and Monica squatted and passed it through her legs.

"Wonderful! Embrace your differences!" Miss Susan clapped.

By the end of the skit, everyone was in stitches. It was the first time Monica had laughed a good laugh since she'd been inside the Ethel Merman.

After a few more improvs, Miss Susan gave each actor notes of things to work on.

"My final message to you is: Learn from each other. Trust each other," Miss Susan said, packing up her things. "You as an actor might be very talented, but you are only as good as the actors around you. So remember to trust each other. Fail, fall, and lift each other up." With that, Miss Susan had them go through a series of trust falls. Everyone had each other's backs, just like they would onstage.

April was giddy after rehearsal that day. "Tomorrow is Halloween, and it's my favorite holiday of all the holidays on Broadway!" she said. Monica hadn't thought much about Halloween. She figured they'd be too busy rehearsing to go trick-or-treating. But before she could ask, April explained that on Broadway, all the theater people go trick-or-treating at the other Broadway theaters.

"The stage doormen hand out the candy, and they get really into it," April said.

"I already have it mapped out." Relly pulled out a piece of paper from his pocket.

"We'll start with the Broadway Theatre on Fifty-Third and make our way down to the New Amsterdam Theatre on Forty-Second," he said, pointing to dots on the page.

"We have to hit the Gershwin early because they hand out huge candy bars!" April commented. "And some of them we can skip because they hand out pencils."

"Okay, the Gershwin first." Relly nodded, still studying the paper.

"What about Halloween costumes?" Monica asked before realizing that was a silly question.

They all smiled at each other and headed to the wardrobe room. There were rows and rows of colorful costumes from past productions. The rest of Sunday afternoon was spent trying on outfits, most of which fit adults. Hudson transformed into a cowboy, April became a chimney sweep, Relly found the perfect 1960s go-go dancing costume, and Monica became a butterfly.

After rehearsal the next day, they headed out with empty pillowcases, intending to hit most of the forty-one theaters on Broadway. At the Gershwin, the stage door-man was ready with a basket of huge candy bars.

"Amazing!" Relly said, wide-eyed.

"You the kids from the Ethel Merman?" the doorman said in a New York accent similar to Jimmy Onions's, handing April the candy.

"We certainly are! How did you know?" April asked, studying the length of the candy bar.

"We doormen know everything that goes on on Broadway."

He gave a candy bar to Relly and Hudson, who quickly moved away toward April to discuss the quickest way to their next stop.

"You Monica?" the doorman asked.

"Yes," Monica said with surprise.

The doorman gave her a wide smile, then got serious, handed her a candy bar, and whispered, "Find it."

Before she could make sense of it, another group of trick-or-treaters was moving in, and her group was moving out.

"Come on," Relly said. "We've got to hurry, before shows go up."

Find it, she thought. The same thing Jimmy Onions had whispered to her.

At the Broadway Theatre, the doorman there offered her a different message. "We believe in you, Monica." At the Neil Simon Theatre, the doorman said, "We're counting on you, kid." At the Richard Rogers Theatre, she got, "You can do it." And it went like that all evening. The other kids didn't pick up on it. Relly was too busy mapping their next hit, April was focused on counting candy, and Hudson was too busy eating it.

As Monica made her way home that evening, still in her butterfly costume, she paced her steps, thinking, *Find it. Find it.* Find what?

Fourteen days until opening night

That Friday, Hudson came to the theater with bags under his eyes. "I've been up baking since three a.m. Anybody else not sleep last night?" he said sluggishly, balancing a large platter of steaming pizza pretzels. "Worrying about my dance moves kept me awake."

He passed behind Relly, who yawned as he stretched his body upward. "I don't know if it's the curse or what, but I feel like my moves look like I'm dancing underwater." He did a simple kick–ball change, which fell flat.

Monica had spent her night wide awake too, in the pitch-black of her hotel room, wondering about the unrelenting power of curses, and the cryptic and encouraging words from the stage doormen. She thought about the conversation she had overheard Artie having with the man in the gray suit, and the mysterious key. And who "the others" were, and what they were doing late at night in the theater. And maybe April was right about the Ethel Merman. Maybe it did suck up superpowers. It hadn't gone unnoticed that April was having trouble remembering her lines, Relly wasn't as crisp with his dance moves, Hudson was forgetful with just about everything, and Monica's voice was not her own.

"All right everyone, stand on the poop. Clap, clap," Maria said, entering the stage with a great deal of seriousness.

"What's the poop?" Monica asked

Hudson leaned over to Monica. "The poop is the deck of a ship. Comes from the French: *la poupe* for 'the stern,' the back of the ship." Hudson scratched his ear. "I think."

There wasn't actually a deck or even a ship yet; the set designers were having trouble building the set, because the curse seemed to take a special interest in hiding or breaking power tools. So Maria used two sawhorses and a stepladder as substitutes. The kids were the only ones who seemed worried about the set not coming together.

"We're going to push through this scene, get through your songs, then end things a little early today," she said.

The kids looked at one another. They had noticed over the last week Maria was not herself either. Usually, she pushed them with harder, longer rehearsals when their technique was lazy or their moves were off. But that had faded into almost . . . joviality when things didn't go right. "Even Maria's thrown in the towel on this production," April would whisper.

"Why are we ending early?" Relly asked.

"Well, Mr. Morton. Good question. We are ending early because all of you are perfectly ready for opening night, so I've decided no more practice needed!" Then she looked squarely at everyone and said in a deep voice, "No, I'm kidding."

She pointed at Relly's feet, at his ballet shoes worn down to the toes. "I can't make proper stars out of you in those old dance slippers. A dancer's language starts in the feet. Lucky for you, the four of you are going to visit my good friend Gino."

Gino Bilcco's modest shoe-making shop was three blocks from the Ethel Merman Theater, wedged between a laundromat and a pizza parlor.

"I can be bossy about shoes," Gino was saying over

the phone, with a laugh, when the four kids arrived. "You can't do the perfect grand jeté eight performances a week in basic loafers."

He raised a finger, signaling to them he'd be off the phone in a moment.

Gino Bilcco's shop was like something out of a fairy tale. It smelled like leather and wood and moss. *Not old Broadway,* Monica thought. *Ancient Broadway.* April pulled out her phone and took a quick group shot. *#newshoesbyGino*

"Ah, now," Gino said, hanging up the phone. "You must be the kids from *Our Time.* I was expecting you a week ago, but Maria said there have been some issues with the production? Hmmmm. Maria's the only person on this planet I'd do a rush job for." He tapped his fingers together, then went around and shook everyone's hands.

"So," he began, putting on an apron and picking up sheets of green pattern paper for tracing their feet, "everyone, remove your footwear! We have important sizing to do. Who'd like to go first?"

They all pointed to Relly, who eagerly took off his shoes and placed his left foot down on the green paper to be traced. Gino's sharp pencil moved smoothly around his foot. Then he scribbled down the measurements, and did the same with Relly's right foot.

On the walls were autographed photos of some of the biggest stars on Broadway.

"You've made shoes for all these people?" Hudson asked.

Gino nodded. "But don't be too impressed. Famous people have bunions and smelly feet just like everyone else."

After he'd measured everyone's feet, he asked the group to do a dance routine so that he could better understand the level of gymnastics the kids would be performing.

"We must make sure that the shoes look simple, but beautiful, of course, and still do their job of giving you the right kind of support," he said. Then he brought out a dance slipper and pointed to parts of the shoe. "We attach the heel to the sole with screws, so not like your average shoe, you know?" Broadway shoes ran the gamut of styles, and it looked like the squad was going to see all of them. "Two straps. One here, the T-strap, and one here, the Mary Jane." They could have a metal bar under the sole, for what was called a fully shanked shoe, or a half shank. Most shoes also had a stublike toe, not a pointed toe, because onstage the foot needed to look normal, not like a chic fashion statement.

"Okay, so now show me part of one of your numbers. Don't mind if I take some notes, please."

The kids pushed the stools aside and agreed to perform the scene where they were leaving the suburbs and heading off to save the Tilt arcade. There was plenty of leaping, and it was one of the more physical routines. As they began, Monica was instantly off, so they started over. Then Relly was off and they started to laugh in embarrassment.

"Sorry, I think we're still learning this one," April said, blushing. They started over and over and over, but they couldn't get it right. "Come on. Together. Together," April repeated, with a redder hue to her face each time.

Gino rubbed his chin. "Maybe try a different scene."

They decided on the opening scene. It was the number they had rehearsed the most. Again, they were off. Gino's original cheerfulness had shifted to a mix of annoyance and pity. Monica wasn't sure which was worse.

"You know what, I think I got what I need. So you say you only have three weeks left until opening night?"

"Two weeks," Hudson said.

"Huh." Gino rubbed his chin again.

April was so frustrated, she picked up her shoes and ran out the shop door onto the busy sidewalk.

The other kids followed shortly after, with their shoes also in their hands.

"We are an embarrassment! I can't go onstage like that!" April said, holding back tears.

"Ever been to the Grand Canyon?" Hudson asked.

"What?" April turned visibly annoyed. "This is no time for joking."

"I'm not joking. I feel like we're at the Grand Canyon. Tied together traveling toward a cliff of disaster."

They all slumped.

"It's like the fortune-teller predicted," April said.

They gave her a funny look.

"The other day, during our lunch break, I went to that fortune-teller around the corner. I should never have gone. I don't even believe in that stuff . . . okay, maybe I do. But I didn't want to believe what she told me."

"What did she tell you?" Hudson asked, slipping on his loafers.

"She said there would be many obstacles in my future if the curse wasn't broken. She actually said the word 'curse.' I hadn't even told her I was an actor or that I was perform-ing at the Ethel Merman. She just knew. Ever since she said that, I have been even more off than I already was. Now I think I'm cursing myself. Like the curse has spread from the Ethel Merman onto me!"

It was now getting close to dusk. They had been in Gino's shop for longer than they'd expected. The lights of the city shone brighter. Theatergoing crowds were begin-ning to gather for dinner before heading to their shows.

As the kids started to walk back to the theater, Monica

happened to look up and stopped dead in her tracks. Her eyes went wide. So wide the other kids tracked where she was looking. It was a billboard across the street. But not just any billboard. All their eyes went wide too.

"The *Our Time* billboard! It's been changed!" Relly said.

"What's Ethel's Equipment?" Hudson knew every inch of New York City and had never heard of that shop.

"So it's true," Monica whispered.

"What's true?" April's hands went on her hips.

"I can't believe it . . . ," Monica said.

"What can't you believe? Do you know something about this?" April said firmly to Monica.

"Several days ago, the day Hudson got stuck in the bathroom, I overheard Artie talking to a man in a suit about turning the Ethel Merman into a luxury hotel. But I didn't think he'd actually do it, at least not *before* our production. I thought . . ." She stopped herself.

The four stood in silence.

"Well, see ya later, good night, good luck, and they all lived happily ever after, the end . . . ," said Hudson, turning to head home.

The three stood in silence. Hudson walked several paces before Monica's face lit up.

"Wait. That's it! And they all lived happily ever after," Monica said with a snap.

The kids looked confused.

"Our show! It's not about telling the story of saving the Tilt arcade. . . ."

"It isn't?" Relly scratched his head.

"No, we're here to tell the story about saving the Ethel Merman!" Monica jumped.

"Mise en abyme," April said with a perfect French accent. "A story within a story."

"Exactly! It's *Our Time*: a group of kids go searching for how to save their subdivision from greedy developers. Except we're also telling the story about saving our theater," Relly said.

"From greedy developers!" they said together.

"But what's the Ethel Merman's story? What was its fall?" Hudson asked.

"You're right, we don't know the story," April said.

"That's what we need to find out," Relly said.

"There's something else I need to tell you." Monica hesitated. "I wasn't sure of it, I thought it was probably nothing . . . but I'm sure of it now." Monica removed the key from her necklace and explained about the mysterious envelope at the front desk of her hotel the night she arrived.

"I thought it was just a key to my dressing room. I didn't even think to try it until this morning when I got to the theater early. It didn't fit the keyhole. Then I tried every door I could find in the Ethel Merman. Nothing. Not even close to a match."

"Did you try the doors in your hotel?" Hudson asked.

"Every single one. Nothing."

"Because that's not a door key. It's for something smaller," Relly said. "And we are going to find out what it is."

Nine

NO ONE PANIC

The kids had split up into two groups. April and Hudson picked the short straw and started on the second floor, then the basement. Relly and Monica got the third and first floors.

"The theater is dark and empty," Relly said in a detective's voice. "We are trapped inside the Ethel Merman Theater." He had pulled out an old-fashioned tape recorder from his backpack and was speaking into it as Monica followed closely behind. She angled the flashlight at his watch.

"We have now been inside the theater for fifty-seven minutes, looking for the mysterious key's lock," Monica said in her own version of a detective's voice. "What does it open, and why? Will we ever find out?" Monica turned to Relly. "What else?"

"The temperature," he said in a whisper.

"Right: the temperature," she repeated, also in a whisper. "It's dropping." They were in the center of the lobby now, determining where to look next.

"What does the coat room have to offer?" Relly recorded. "What could be under the stairs?" They passed a mirror, and, catching his reflection, he noted: "Why is Relly Morton so devilishly handsome?"

Monica laughed. Relly had many talents, but Monica decided that his ability to find humor in stressful situations was one of his greatest talents of all. She could learn a thing or two from him. Suddenly, the lights, which had been off, started to flicker on. They both felt an eerie sensation surround them; the room felt even colder.

"There's a presence here," Monica whispered to Relly.

"I feel it too." He was slightly alarmed by the lights flickering, but he didn't show his fear to Monica. "They're just lights—they go on and off from time to time. Old theaters," Relly said to assure both himself and Monica.

Monica nodded. "I'm going to go look in the orchestra pit," she said.

Right as Monica left, Relly suddenly heard a ghostly voice say: "Adventure is always in store!"

Relly was a logical person: there were no such things as ghosts. Maybe certain energies that grew in intensity from time to time, but actual floating sheets? Naw. He shook his head to rid himself of the image. But he heard it again: "Never say *die*!" This time, the voice was louder, closer. A finger tapped his shoulder, and Relly clutched his recorder but dropped his flashlight. Relly screamed and realized it was April, who screamed too. Somewhere in the distance a faint scream came from within the theater. It was Monica.

"April, did you see it? I think it was a ghost talking to me."

"Was it saying 'Adventure is always in store'?" asked April.

"Yes!"

April rolled her eyes. "That was me, silly. I was channeling *Our Time*."

Adventure is always in store was the motto the kids would repeat throughout the show.

"I knew that . . . ," Relly said, embarrassed at how obvious it should have been.

Monica raced back. "Maybe we could search the orchestra pit together."

"I still don't get why we had to split up," Hudson said through heavy breaths. He'd come from the basement shortly behind April.

"Did you find anything in the front of the house?" April asked Relly and Monica.

"Nothing in the lobby, the coatroom, or the stairs leading to the balcony level. You find anything?" Relly asked.

"Nothing," said Hudson.

No mystery keyholes anywhere. They slumped down on the stairs, discouraged, exhausted, and hungry.

"You win, Ethel!" April said to the golden Ethel statue at the top of the stairs, frozen in its glorious pose of joy.

They sat for a moment; then they all turned and looked at the Ethel Merman statue.

They kept their eyes on it for several beats. Monica cocked her head. Hudson cocked his head. Relly leaned toward it with a furrowed brow. April's mouth fell open.

"The Ethel Merman statue!" they said together.

They scrabbled up the stairs toward it.

April reread Ethel Merman's quote:

"'Be yourself; it's the one thing you can do better than anyone else.'"

"Is it a clue?" Relly asked.

"I think it's just good advice." Hudson moved closer. "Maybe her arms move." They didn't.

"Or her foot." April tried to twist. Nothing.

They looked top to toe for anything that resembled a keyhole.

The wind started to blow outside.

Nothing on the statue shifted or moved or seemed unusual.

"What's this?" Monica said, examining the lettering of the quotation. "Relly, shine your light a little closer."

In the quote written on the plaque underneath the statue, the *B* in the word "Be" looked slightly odd, with two notches cut into the bronze. "It's a keyhole. *The* keyhole!" Monica quickly grabbed for the small golden key around her neck. Her hands trembled as her fingers searched for the clasp. Nervousness. Excitement. Fear. She had a flash of Freddy, her parents, her abuelita. She shoved fear down, pinched the clasp, threaded the key off her lucky chain, and went straight for the lock.

Relly held the light like he was holding a fire hose. "Go!" The lights in the theater flickered, and a rumbling of thunder outside was accompanied by flashes of lightning that blinked through different windows like an arcade game. In an instant, the theater felt like a howling wilderness. She slid the key in and it clicked into place.

She drew a long, deep breath and squared her eyes at the words "Be yourself" before twisting. The lock was attached to a door, which opened to a little compartment of blackness. Monica's hand went in and came out with a small, white piece of folded paper. She held it for a moment like a precious gift. Her body shook.

"Who wants to read it?" she asked.

"You read it. The key was given to you!" April said.

Relly aimed his light onto the stark white paper. Monica opened the note intently, unfolding each layer with care, and finally, after what seemed like an eternity, looked at the words. She crouched with a puzzled look on her face, the note wide open in her palms like a world laid flat.

"What does it say?" everyone asked anxiously.

Relly's flashlight cast an eerie shadow under Monica's face.

"It says, 'Happy Birthday,'" Monica said with confusion.

The wind outside eased; the lights stopped flickering. Relly inspected the note, the handwriting, the color of the ink, the paper. The handwriting wasn't familiar. "Standard chicken scratch," Relly said. The paper and ink seemed fresh.

"Is it your birthday?" he asked.

"Not until June," Monica said.

"Is it any one of our birthdays?" April asked. It wasn't.

"Is this some kind of joke?" Hudson said loudly, looking at the frozen Ethel statue.

They slumped back on the stairs. A good long minute passed, almost a lifetime for April to have not said one single word, but their current situation left even her speechless. Then they heard a rustling sound.

"What was that?" whispered Relly, flicking off his flashlight to hide their presence. They heard sounds of movement. The kids sat frozen in the pitch-blackness, too afraid to move, scream, or even turn their heads ever-so-slightly to look at one another. All their expressions were the same: stone-cold fear.

Hudson whispered, "I told you this place was haunted." A thud. Then another. The kids jumped. Something was happening in the auditorium. Onstage.

"Let's go see." April led them quietly toward the back of the auditorium to get a better look.

The ghost light had been turned off and placed to the side of the stage. A shadow crept. Then there was a click, click, click, and mumbling. The shadow bent over. Click, click, click again. Then a small light appeared. The clicking was a lighter lighting a candle. Then several candles of varying heights were placed in the middle of the stage. Another shadow moved in, carrying a chair. Then another, with two chairs. They formed a tight circle of a dozen chairs around the center of candles. The chairs filled with shadows in the silence. It was strange and beautiful.

The original shadow spoke.

"Welcome back," the female voice said calmly.

It was hard for the kids to hear, so they edged closer without being seen.

The voice continued to talk, but it was difficult for the kids to make out what she was saying.

"Wait, is that Amanda's voice?" April whispered.

They edged even closer, and now they could make out faces. It was Amanda, the original shadow. Next to her was Maria. Also in the circle were a few adult actors from the cast, Chris from the wig room, Miss Susan, and a couple of musicians from the orchestra.

"Even Mr. Fernando?" Relly said. It was hard to comprehend.

Those onstage held hands as Amanda led them in soft chanting.

"It's a séance!" Relly said eagerly. He held his recorder toward the voices. "But I can't tell what they're saying."

Then came humming, like fingers moving around crystal glasses.

"They're channeling the spirit of the Ethel Merman," Relly guessed.

"Or spirits," Hudson said.

The chanting and humming lasted for ten minutes. Then they sat silently. Nothing happened.

Then, as quietly as they had arrived, they got up, removed the chairs, blew out the candles, placed the ghost light back in its spot and turned it on. Then the adults left.

"What is going on?" April asked.

The kids looked at one another without being able to answer the question.

"Nothing happened," Hudson said.

They went onstage to examine things further. The waterfall had a slight trickle.

"Meh," Hudson said. "Did they think a séance would get the waterfall to work?"

"Can someone please tell me what's up with the waterfall anyway?" Monica said, a little annoyed.

"Ah, the waterfall saga," Hudson began with a professorial tone. "So long ago, yet so very very recent."

"The second day we arrived for rehearsal," April started, "when Tabitha was still here, there was a fire in the wig room. We were rehearsing onstage with Maria when Chris came running onstage yelling that the wigs were on fire."

Relly chimed in, "Then the sprinklers onstage went off. Then all the sprinklers in the entire theater went off, just from one little curling iron. We had to evacuate the building, and two fire trucks came."

"It was actually kind of exciting for our first week," April said, then paused. "We didn't know about the curse then, and we didn't know what would follow."

Hudson continued: "The fire was contained quickly—a few wigs were destroyed. But"—Hudson hung on the word for a moment—"just as the fire marshal walked out of the theater to declare the place safe, *boom!*"

Relly shook his head. "The waterfall saga."

"What was the boom?" Monica asked.

"A bunch of buckets on the fly system filled with water from the sprinklers. They were on pulleys, and the weight of the water pulled down the buckets, which somehow managed to dislodge an eight-hundred-pound ballast from the rig," said Relly.

Monica didn't quite understand.

"The ballast landed right on the perfectly working, gleaming, shiny new waterfall just brought in from Chicago."

"No!" Monica said.

"Yes." Hudson shivered.

"Nobody," Relly whispered, "not even the fire marshal, had ever seen anything like it. There was no explanation for how six small buckets of water could take down an eight-hundred-pound ballast."

"Artie's face," Hudson said with sadness, "it was white. Pale as a ghost."

"He didn't think the curse would affect his production. He thought we would escape it and save the theater. But he knew in that moment that this curse was going to bring him down," April said.

"And everyone else with him," Relly finished.

"A week later, Tabitha was gone, and things went downhill from there," Hudson said.

The lights flickered again.

Something groaned nearby.

"It's just the wind," Monica said firmly. But she wasn't sure she even believed herself.

On her way home from the theater, Monica called Marissa and told her everything. The curse, the accidents, the mystery key, the birthday message.

"Mo, that's out of a movie! Have you told your abuelita?" Marissa asked.

"No," Monica replied.

"Why not?"

"I don't want to upset her. She's so excited about my Broadway debut. I think it would crush her spirit to know the theater is cursed."

There was a long pause on the other end.

Then Marissa said, "It's kind of weird, isn't it?"

"What is?"

"That this curse thing is happening to you," Marissa answered.

"What do you mean, happening *to me*?" Monica sounded offended.

"You know, with your family's history and everything," Marissa said.

"What do you mean, my family's history?"

"Oh, um . . ." Marissa paused.

"What do you mean, my family's history!" Monica repeated.

"It's just a story your father once told my father. I don't really know much about it."

"Well, tell me what you *do* know," Monica said firmly.

Thirteen days until opening night
"I checked three things off my bucket list yesterday," Monica's abuelita said Saturday morning as she poured hot water into Styrofoam cups of instant oatmeal. Monica smiled, but she wasn't really listening.

"First I went down to Wall Street. Then I visited Chinatown, got you and your brother a few souvenirs." She pointed to a full bag next to the sleeper sofa. "And then I went to Coney Island in Brooklyn and rode the Cyclone!"

"Oh, that sounds fun," Monica said in a monotone voice, staring at her oatmeal.

Monica's abuelita put down the hot water and studied her granddaughter.

"I'm going to take you there so you can ride the roller coaster, too."

"I'd love that."

"How about today?"

Monica wasn't in the mood to talk about roller coasters.

"Kita, what is the matter?"

"I'm just tired. Long rehearsal yesterday. And another one today."

"So tell me why you have to be at rehearsal another entire weekend and not ride roller coasters with your abuelita."

Monica shrugged.

"Why don't you tell me something about the show instead of shrugging your shoulders all the time."

Monica wasn't ready to share with her abuelita that their hopes for a Broadway hit would soon be dashed.

Monica's abuelita sat patiently. She scooped oatmeal into her mouth, studying her granddaughter as she ate.

"Mr. Fernando, my voice coach, he reminds me of Sean."

This made her abuelita smile. Sean was Reedley's friendliest mailman. He left little chocolates for the kids and dog bones for the dogs.

"Well, I'm glad Mr. Fernando is nice."

"Abuelita?"

"Yes?" she said, wiping her mouth.

"Our Freddy jar."

Her abuelita turned to look at the half-filled jar.

"Not bad. New York has a lot of shiny change on the ground."

"Loose change won't pay for Freddy's surgery, will it?"

"No, it won't." Her abuelita took another bite of oatmeal. She chewed quietly.

Monica's eyes got serious. She looked right at her abuelita and said, "Tell me about the goat men."

Her abuelita stopped chewing and set down her spoon. She sat back in her chair.

They sat quietly for a moment, studying each other.

"Please, Abuelita, tell me," Monica said.

It was an old story. A family story. One that was only talked about in hushed tones.

"Yes, Kita. I thought you might want to hear it someday." Her abuelita removed her large round glasses and cleaned them with a hankie, then put them back on. "And now is a good day for it." The glasses slid down her nose.

"Long, long ago, my great-grandfather's village near Puebla, in Mexico, became cursed. Just like your theater." Monica looked at her. Her abuelita smiled. She had sensed it from the very first moment she saw the Ethel Merman.

"It started when a pack of wolves came down from the cold mountains in search of food. They would steal the village goats in the middle of the night. This went on for several weeks. Finally, the strong young men gathered to hunt for the destructive wolves. My father, your great-grandfather, stayed behind. He was of middle age, but still too old to go climbing around in the mountains in the dark. He and the other older men and women in the village played dominoes and tended to the children and waited patiently for news of the men. The younger women cooked big meals in preparation for a celebration upon their return. But the strong men were gone many days, and the villagers worried they would never be seen again. Finally, a week later, they came down from the mountains, wide-eyed and bleating like goats. Goats!"

Monica's eyes settled on the small sink of their hotel room. A drop of water hung from the faucet, then dripped into the basin without a sound.

Her abuelita continued, "The villagers could not understand what had happened to them. Then a mysterious woman wearing a green dress, the color of moss, came down the mountain path. She said she'd been angered by the men's intention to hunt her wolves. The men had tried to harm the mountain's beautiful creatures, and for that

they must pay. The men were sent to their beds to rest."
Monica's abuelita paused, taking in her granddaughter's
reaction.

"Then what happened, Abuelita?"

"The village's *curandera* . . ." Her abuelita stopped.

"Witch doctor!" Monica said.

"She was a healer, Kita. People would travel from all
over Mexico to seek her advice."

"Cursed people?"

"People went to her for all sorts of things. If you didn't
have an appetite, she would rub an egg on your stomach
and bid the evil spirits away. If something scared you, she
would make you lie down on the ground and pass a brush
full of leaves over you. Her spirit still travels with me."

"Why with you?"

"Because she was mi mamá. Su bisabuela."

"Elvia?"

"Yes."

"Mi bisabuela was a village curandera?"

"She wasn't just a village curandera. She was a very
powerful woman. Do you remember her at all?"

"Oh yes." Monica shivered.

Her abuelita let out one loud laugh. "She could be
very mysterious when she wanted to be. Imagine having a
curandera for a mother when you didn't clean your room!"

By the time Monica knew her, Elvia could only see out of one eye and walked bent over, and whenever Monica got close to her, she would say, "Ayyyy, Kiiiitaaaa," and Monica would run away.

"What did she do about the goat men?" Monica asked.

"Su bisabuela tried everything. She fed the goat men potions and herbs. She rubbed special lotions on their ears and temples. She said prayers and gathered the villagers to chant around them—"

"Like a séance?" Monica interrupted.

"The word *séance* comes from the French for sitting quietly. So, yes, I suppose it was like that. She would sit and call to the spirit world to banish the evil from their village."

"Did the sitting work?"

"No."

"So the men stayed like goats forever?"

"After a month, their eyes were still wild and their hair grew long. They continued to talk in the language of goats. The villagers had grown tired, exhausted with worry and fear. Fear spread the witch's spell throughout the village. Houses began to burn, and sudden drought destroyed their crops. People went hungry and thirsty. Soon the village was cursed."

"The entire village?"

"Yes."

"So what did they do to de-curse the men and the village?"

Her abuelita thought long and hard before she answered.

"Monica, you can't break a curse when you live in fear of it. I was nine years old when the men came down from the mountain speaking in goat tongues. We were full of fear."

Monica had seen a picture of her abuelita at that age. She was standing in front of her family's pink house. It was the last photo they took before they left the village for good.

Monica's abuelita got up and cleared the barely touched Styrofoam cups. She went over to the window that looked out onto the wall next door.

"I never went back to the village after we left. But I'm told times got harder. The spirits became too strong. Eventually the village surrendered."

"Surrendered?"

"Yes, my girl."

"What do you mean?"

"Sometimes you have to hold the spirit, the curse, inside you. Then you have to release it. Sometimes it's very difficult to get it out." Monica studied the deep lines on her abuelita's face. "The village slowly turned into a pasture for goats."

"And Elvia?"

"She came to California in her final years. When you met her, she was not much older than the age I am now, but she looked one hundred years old. She had internalized the curse, and eventually it wore her down." She gave Monica a look full of meaning. "Your theater . . . people are afraid. Things are off balance."

"What do you mean?"

"You know the Ojo de Dios that your great-abuelita gave you?" The one Monica had hanging at the theater. "God's eyes were originally made by the Huichol people of Mexico. The four points represent fire, earth, air, and water—the four elements that make up everything on our planet. When they aren't balanced, everything is off. The center is the 'eye'—the portal to the spirit world. The elements are not aligned. It was the same for our little village."

Monica sent a text to April on her way to the theater that morning: We have to stop the curse from ruining the show.

April texted back immediately: Yes!

Followed by another text: How?

Monica answered: I have a plan.

Interlude

"Jump"

Don't be afraid
To jump!
Just follow me!
And jump!
Count one, two, three!
The map has led us here
So let go of all fear
We're not sure what's ahead
But we know if we stay here, we'll all be
dead

So I'll see you on the other side, my friends
till the end
This has been one crazy ride, and it's only
just begun
Who'd have thought we would be on this
chase?
But we have to go now, 'cause, you guys, it's
too late

To go home with nothing to show

We got this moment right now

Just let go!

Don't be afraid

To jump!

Just follow me!

And jump!

Count one, two, three!

The map has led us here

So let go of all fear

We're not sure what's ahead

But we know if we stay here, we're dead

Ten

THE PLAN

The kids met in Monica and April's dressing room first thing that morning. April slid a red marker across another day on the calendar. "Thirteen days." The girls' dressing room was on the second floor of the theater. Even though it was down the hall a ways, it got very little privacy. They needed to talk quickly and quietly before others started to arrive.

"So what's your plan?" April whispered to Monica.

"Is it a séance? I think we should do a séance." Relly rubbed his hands as if he were about to sink his teeth into a big meal.

"Yeah, but one that works," Hudson chimed in.

"Rise, ghosts of the Ethel Merman, and be heard!" Relly lifted his whole body toward the leaky ceiling.

"No. Not a séance." Monica had a playful smile on her face. An easy kind of friendship had formed among the four kid actors over the past couple of weeks.

"My plan is . . ." Monica paused, went to the door, and leaned out to make sure it was just them. "My plan is," she repeated more quietly, "to give up."

"Huh?" Relly said.

"That's your plan?" April looked deflated.

Hudson stopped eating his banana.

A silence fell among the four. April sank down into a puffy chair. It ballooned out for a second before the shape settled underneath her. She studied the Broadway posters on the wall. Suddenly it all seemed for nothing. Actors were replaceable; everyone knew that. One flop and you were at the bottom of everyone's wish list.

"Sure, why not? Giving up is as much of an option as not giving up, right?" Monica smiled smugly. "We don't have to continue. We can just give up."

"No!" Hudson said firmly. "I've been performing in off-Broadway and off-off-Broadway productions for my whole career. One audition after another after another of rejection. Finally I get here. Here! Broadway, and as a lead! Do you know how many Broadway roles there are for big-boned kids with two left feet? Not many. I'm not giving this up, not for nothing," he said, shaking his head. "At least, I'm not giving up until Artie officially says he's shutting down the show." The others nodded, agreeing with his stance.

Monica walked over to her dressing table, looked at herself squarely in the mirror, and said, "Good. That was a test." Turning to them, she continued, with deep, intense eyes, "Because for this plan to work, we all need to be in this together. One hundred percent. Got it?"

They observed her, half in surprise, half in awe. Monica wasn't that same shy girl who'd just stepped off an airplane less than two weeks earlier. She had a sort of finesse. She'd nearly forgotten that she was the understudy to the understudy.

"I got my start singing in malls," Monica said. She supposed she wouldn't have felt comfortable telling the others that when she first arrived, but maybe a little bit of April was rubbing off on her. "Everyone gets their start somewhere," April could be heard saying on occasion.

"My abuelita would drive me to a crowded mall on a weekend afternoon, and I'd find a spot that looked like it could be a good stage, and I'd sing with a boom box and a Barbie microphone and a gold sequined top hat that my mom bought from the local dance school. Sometimes four or five people would stop and listen; a few times I got much bigger audiences."

"My first gig was for a baby diaper commercial," Hudson said casually.

"Here's my plan." Monica scribbled something on a piece of blank paper. She held it up: *Come See* Our Time *and Be Part of Broadway's Magic!* The others looked confused. "A promotional flyer."

"We're going to sing in malls and pass out flyers?" Hudson asked.

"Yes! Guerrilla marketing!" Relly said, pumping his fist. Unconventional tactics to advertise their show using a small budget—in their case, no budget.

"We are completely off schedule as it is now," April pointed out. "How are we going to find time to do this?"

"I guess April has a point. We don't even know any of the dance routines all the way through yet," Hudson said.

"Yes and no," Monica said calmly. "We can perform in front of crowds after rehearsals. It'll be extra hours of practice time."

April lifted herself off the chair enthusiastically and said, "What do we have to lose. Let's do it! With sold-out shows, Artie will have to keep the production running."

"When do we start?" Relly asked.

"Tomorrow after rehearsal," Monica said.

They all agreed.

"So that's how we're going to get rid of the curse?" Hudson asked.

"No. That's about saving the show. We can't break the curse on the theater if we don't have a show to perform. There's another part to the plan." Monica reached over and held the god's eye that was hanging from her mirror. "We need to figure out what's cursing the Ethel Merman. It is our duty," Monica said.

"We don't have much to go on," Relly reminded her.

"Jimmy Onions knows something, and we need to find out what." Monica smiled.

Jimmy was sitting in his usual spot at the stage door. He was having his lunch for breakfast and watching the news on a small TV.

"Covering another Saturday shift?" Monica said.

"And my card buddies are none too happy," Jimmy said.

"Do you believe in life after death?" Relly asked Jimmy. The other three gave Relly a strange look. That was some conversation starter.

"Sure, kid. Guess we all gotta go someplace when we're not in this place," Jimmy said matter-of-factly.

There were a few clues about Jimmy's personal life in his cubby office: he had a wife and two grown sons, and a bunch of grandchildren who liked the beach. A stack of joke books and a dance trophy that looked decades old sat on a small shelf above him, and he had a corner dedicated to his magic-trick supplies.

"Why do you ask?"

"Amanda assigned us to interview a person in the theater each day this week. You're our interview for the day!" April jumped in nervously.

"I'm honored. What else you got?"

Hudson went next. "So, uh, how long have you been working here?"

"Forty-four years. Best forty-four of my life."

He lifted his lapel to show off his security badge:

James Lorenzo
44 years of service

Relly took notes. "What's one of your favorite features of the Ethel Merman Theater?" Relly asked.

"The Ethel Merman has the oldest pipe organ on all of Broadway. One hundred sixty-eight pipes, all still in working condition. It's a beaut."

"And what's been your most memorable moment here?" Monica asked.

"That's easy. When Carol Channing walked through

this very door for the first time to star in *Hello, Dolly!* and said, 'Don't freeze on me now, but I need you to tell me where I can powder my nose.' She was her own creation, that one. True balladeer, you know?"

The kids looked at one another. Monica twisted her hair. Relly continued to ask questions.

"What about the curse thing. Do you believe that stuff?" Relly asked casually.

Jimmy thought for a moment. Looked at the little TV, grabbed a cracker, and held it.

"Thing of it is, yeah, I do. Started getting weird around here . . . well, it must be twenty-five years ago now. I remember it was twenty-five years, because it was right around when the Yankees won the World Series and all of New York City felt lucky because they'd broken their losing streak of almost twenty years. That was the year all the lights in the city glowed brighter. But in the Ethel Merman, that's when the lights started to flicker and the doors started to slam shut. Same time that was going on, the theater started to lose money. More and more productions were ending up flops. Didn't happen quickly. Happened real slow. You know? So as no one really knew it here until it was too late." He looked at the TV.

"What was your question?" Jimmy asked.

The buzzer to the stage door sounded. Maria walked in.

"Oh, my adoring fans have come to greet me, I see. How nice of you," Maria said with a clap. "You must be eager to get started on something new!"

The kids looked at one another with smiles.

Twelve days until opening night

Monica pulled her finger along the gleaming marble that surrounded the ice rink in the sunken plaza of Rockefeller Center. She looked up at the bronze gilded statue of what looked like a floating man with his arms held in the air.

"The Titan Prometheus," Hudson pointed out. "Brought fire to man."

Monica studied the statue for a long time. Then she looked around the plaza. One of the first photographs Monica had ever seen of New York City had been taken there. It was that famous old black-and-white photograph of eleven construction workers sitting way above the city on a steal beam casually relaxing during their lunch break. They were building Rockefeller Center. And now here she was.

Relly said, "Come on, let's set up over here." He had found a spot near a group of happy tourists taking photographs.

It was late afternoon, and even though it was relatively warm out for November, the ice rink only lasted for the winter season and was packed with people. In April, the rink would be gone, magically transformed into a restaurant. Monica watched as skaters twirled and stumbled around on the ice. She smiled, thinking what it must feel like to glide on ice.

The kids were in their street clothes. Relly had set up a basic sound system.

April began in a booming voice: "Four Broadway kids hit Rockefeller Center! Hello, everyone! We're the kid cast of *Our Time*. Less than two weeks away from opening night, and we wanted to give you a preview of our hot new show!"

Most people passed by with nothing more than a glance.

"Keep going," Monica whispered. She knew it took time to gather a crowd.

"Cue the music," April said.

Relly turned on the music, and a small group of teenagers stopped to watch. They took a few photos. The kids had only just begun their routine when they were interrupted by a woman in a nice-looking business suit.

"You kids are great! I'm a huge Broadway fan." She handed the kids her business card. "Paula Williams, producer at *Rise and Shine* here at Thirty Rock. Mind if I get my camera crew out here for a song? I'd love to film a segment for tomorrow morning's show."

Within minutes, two cameramen arrived with a microphone on a boom and a couple of lights. Attracted by the cameras, a large crowd of people formed around them. The producer spoke to a reporter who would introduce them and then ask a few questions about the production.

"Ready and . . ." Relly clicked on the music for the second time that day, and the four fanned out. They went around the tight circle of people clapping their hands and encouraging others to clap along with them. Relly did a backflip, and people began to cheer.

The squad started to sing in perfect harmony, dance in perfect unison. They gave one another sideways glances of surprise, considering they hadn't had a good rehearsal in a while!

Maria's choreography for the number was a blend of hip-hop and ballet. They completed their partner cartwheels, something they'd been having trouble with, exactly right. Their confidence grew, as did their dance moves. Hudson spontaneously performed an incredible breakdancing windmill into a backspin. He whipped around in a circle, landing on his side, and gave a thumbs up to the audience. The crowd went wild.

"I'm not even sure what just happened!" April said afterward. They had been stars, individually and together.

The kids signed autographs and posed for photos.

"All of New York loves us!" Hudson proclaimed.

Monica still couldn't believe what had just happened. Maybe things would actually be okay.

Eleven

A FIELD TRIP

Eleven days until opening night

Their performance made it onto national television the next morning. Within hours, they had over a million views of their performance on social media. It took Artie, who wasn't much for answering telephone calls, until the afternoon to figure out what was going on. In the meantime, back at the Ethel Merman, it was business as usual. No one seemed to be aware of the incredible feat they just accomplished. Not the stagehands, not Jimmy Onions, not Artie.

"Hello, hello, ladles and jelly spoons!" Amanda danced into the classroom carrying her usual half-eaten hot dog in one hand, an umbrella in the other. The kids stood where they were. They had a lot of questions. Like how exactly she was involved with the curse of the Ethel Merman.

"Fractions today," she said with an expression of feigned delight.

"Is it raining outside?" April asked. "I had a sunny drive in from New Jersey."

"Oh no," she said, laughing, looking at her umbrella. "Just in case we get a little wet inside the Ethel Merman today." She took a huge bite of her hot dog.

The kids looked at one another.

"We were wondering, Amanda," said April. "What is our school policy on field trips?"

Amanda paused.

April continued, "Instead of fractions today, a lot of us are interested in learning about the history of Broadway. We were so inspired by your tour—dissection—of the Ethel Merman that first day that some of us would like to learn more."

Amanda blushed. "Well, thank you."

April continued, already knowing the answer to her question. "Is there a library in New York that has that information? You had mentioned something about a Performing Arts Library when you were giving us a tour of the theater."

This was a trick. The kids needed an adult escort.

"Well, we really should stick with the schedule today. But in this case—oh, let's throw caution to the wind!"

Amanda took one last bite of her hot dog before almost skipping out of the theater.

New York's Library for the Performing Arts was a bit of a hike from the Ethel Merman. But anything anyone ever wanted to know about Broadway was in that library.

"They have the largest dance archive in the world," Amanda said, leading them down the street like a drum major as she wove past strollers and dawdling tourists. "And many other archives, on basically everything theater. Oh, we could take a guided tour! They have those. This library is truly *truly* contagious."

When they got to the library, they were greeted by a display of Olivier Awards and Tony Awards. April put her hand on the glass. "You and me, Tony. So close." They browsed the costume section, props, music. Amanda was doing her tour-guide thing again, chatting away about what the library was normally used for.

"You really know your way around," Hudson said.

"Yes! I was here just the other day, in fact. Which reminds me, I need to check on a book I placed on hold."

This was their chance.

"We don't have much time," Relly waved them in the direction they needed to go, pointing to an entire row of filing cabinets. "History of Broadway Theaters," he said.

They all huddled around a narrow filing cabinet.

"Hurry up," April said, leaning in as Hudson pulled the handle.

"I'm hurrying," Hudson said, and pushed out his elbows. "Space."

"Want me to do it?" April tried to push Hudson to the side.

"Guys! Please." Monica elbowed her way in as well. "Just do it quickly, Hudson."

The theaters were listed in alphabetical order.

"Booth, Cort, Eugene O'Neill, Gershwin . . ." Hudson was flipping fast.

"You passed it," Relly said.

Hudson went back and looked. "Here it is. The Ethel Merman."

He pulled out the thinnest file in the cabinet.

"This?" they all said together.

The file offered very little in the way of clues: all the productions, several actors' biographies, a few notable moments. Tons of articles on its flops.

"Nothing about a curse." Hudson slumped back onto his ankles.

"Strange, the file only goes back to the 1990s . . . ," Relly said.

"That's when Jimmy said the curse started," April noted.

"So someone stole the information leading up to the curse?" Monica said.

"Why would anybody do that?" April asked.

"So we couldn't get our hands on it," Hudson said.

"Maybe they're protecting the curse," Monica said.

"Maybe someone doesn't want to stop the curse from ruining the theater!" Relly concluded, putting his finger to his chin.

Relly took a few photos of information from the file. Then they heard Amanda coming and quickly replaced the file.

"What do we do now?" Hudson said.

No one knew. It was a dead end.

"Best get back to the theater!" Amanda poked her head around the corner, book in hand.

As they were leaving, Monica thought of something, and with a quick turn said to Amanda, "I almost forgot." The other kids were way ahead of them. "I need to look up some information for my abuelita. She's a huge Lin-Manuel Miranda fan."

"I can wait," Amanda said, pausing her step.

"No, I'll just catch up with you in a bit. I know my way back to the theater," Monica said, turning to head back inside before Amanda had time to challenge her.

"I really don't mind waiting," Amanda called to her.

"And cut into rehearsal time?" Monica said.

Amanda cocked her head. "Good point."

"I won't be long," she said, and skipped off.

Monica was curious about something. Who was Ethel Merman? Funny, yes. Big voice. Her abuelita sang her songs at home. "It's De-Lovely" was one of her favorites. Monica and Freddy knew the refrain:

The night is young, the skies are clear
And if you want to go walking, dear
It's delightful, it's delicious, it's de-lovely.

She could hear her brother singing along with her abuelita, and it made her smile. Then she got serious again.

"How did Ethel Merman get a theater named after her?" Monica said to herself. Maybe she held some clues about the curse. Monica headed to the Actors' Biographies section.

Ethel's biography file was thick. Monica was sitting cross-legged on the floor, looking through it, when a voice sounded above her. "Ethel Merman was considered the First Lady of Broadway, you know."

Monica paused. She'd been caught. But then, wait. She recognized the voice. It was Amanda's. She turned her head slowly.

"I didn't mean to startle you," Amanda said, with her

usual soft face and bright smile. "But I figured you'd come back looking for clues."

"I was just . . . um . . ." Monica twisted her hair, her other hand placed flat on the Ethel Merman file wide open on the floor. How did Amanda know?

"Do you want to know why Ethel Merman was one of the greats?" Amanda asked. Before Monica could answer, she continued. "She wasn't the typical Broadway actress in her day. People said she was too loud. Too brash."

Amanda reached down for the file. A photograph of Ethel slid out. Amanda picked it up and studied it.

"She was one of the hardest-working women on Broadway. And she had no fear." Amanda looked at Monica. She repeated: "She had *no* fear." Putting down the photo, she asked, "Is this why you came back?"

"Yes." Monica wanted to say more, but shyness had taken over. "My abuelita really liked her, so . . ."

"I should confess, I really liked her too." Amanda smiled.

The two looked down at the file.

"I have another confession." Amanda got uncharacteristically serious. Monica steadied herself. "I'd actually been to the Ethel Merman many times before. When I was younger."

Monica knew it!

"Although back then it was known as the Ogden, not the Ethel Merman."

Monica's eyes widened. The Ogden Theater? Amanda hadn't mentioned this during her tour. Had she?

It clicked. The kids had been looking in the wrong file.

"See you back at the theater," Amanda said with a wink.

With that, Amanda stood up straight, pulled down on her shirt to remove the wrinkles, and left.

Monica had just enough time to photocopy the Ogden Theater file and get back before anybody noticed she'd been gone too long. She couldn't wait to tell April, Relly, and Hudson.

They were going to break the curse.

They were going to save the Ethel Merman.

They were going to save the show.

They were going to be stars on Broadway.

Freddy was going to get his surgery.

Monica raced to the theater. She rang for Jimmy at the stage door. Nothing.

"Jimmy! Jimmy!" She rang the bell again. Her heart was racing. She had butterflies.

After half a minute, which seemed like an eternity, Jimmy opened the door without a smile. When he saw her, he didn't say hello, either—he immediately looked up, as if looking at the penny above the door, then down at his shoes. That was strange. But Monica couldn't help but feel giddy, even if Jimmy was having an off day. And he still didn't say a word even when she asked where the others were. *What has the curse done now?* she thought.

As she walked through the hall toward the stage, the entire theater was quiet. It felt more like church than Broadway. Even the sound guys didn't wave to her. They just looked down. She saw April.

"April! Oh my gosh, I have to tell you something! Where is everybody else?" But April could barely look at her either. Relly came over and gave her a hug. Hudson said, "Sorry, Monica."

What was going on?

She walked closer to the stage. Artie was there, and so was Maria, Amanda, Mr. Fernando, and Hugh's understudy. And there was someone else. Someone new. Someone with long auburn hair.

"Who's that?" Monica whispered.

No one answered her question at first. So she repeated herself: "Will someone please talk to me?"

"That's Tabitha Fox," Hudson said after some silence.

Tabitha turned around. She was tall. Confident. Strong. The kind of actress who could probably belt to the back of the theater and across the street.

Tabitha flashed a dazzling smile. Her eyes brightened.

"Oh, is this who's been taking my place while I was away?" Tabitha flashed another smile. "Thank you!" she said to Monica.

She returned to rehearsing.

What just happened? Monica thought. Her heart was beating out of her chest. She thought she was going to burst into tears right in front of everyone. She grabbed her hair and twisted and said to herself, *Don't cry. Don't cry.*

"It turns out, all the publicity from the morning show stirred newfound interest in the production for Tabitha," Artie said a little sheepishly. Truthfully, he couldn't resist having his star lead back—even if she didn't know any of the dance routines. "Opening night is sold out. So are several weeks after that." He decided not to say anything more. There was an awkward silence.

Everyone wanted to see the show that was blessed with talent and cursed with risk. Tabitha knew all eyes would be on her. If she could pull off a top performance amid all the wreckage, the rest of her career would be golden. Plus, she brought much-needed star power to the production, which made Artie giddy.

"Monica," Maria called out, breaking the silence and moving the rehearsal along. "You'll be with the understudies today. Studio B."

Monica looked at everyone onstage. They all looked

down. Except for Amanda. Amanda looked straight at her with a kind of fire in her eyes. The silly, breezy woman was gone. Amanda studied Monica and gave her one firm nod.

Monica walked to her dressing room. Tabitha had already set Monica's few things outside in the hall. The god's eye still hung on the dressing-room mirror. Monica decided to leave it, for luck. Clearly luck was needed now, more than ever.

Interlude

"Above It All"

They say one is the loneliest number
But they never tell you 'bout three
You're only asked to speak your mind
When the other two can't agree

You learn to say, "It's cool"
when they forget you're there
But there's something you just want to
share

Someday it would be great to get the first
call
And one day they'll think I'm the best of
them all

'Cause my jokes are better than anyone
around
And when you tell me a secret, I won't make
a sound

FEARLESS

I don't want to be a second thought in
anybody's mind

I wanna matter to you
But most of all to me
And I'll tell you the truth
When I see things you just can't see

'Cause I'm the best friend that you never
knew you needed. . . .

Twelve

THE HEARTS OF TREES

That evening, Monica sat on the fire escape, breathing in the sensation of East Coast cold. November brought with it a kind of chill she had never felt in California. She decided a person needed to mentally prepare for this kind of weather. Monica pulled her sweater over her shoulders and listened for sounds from the street below. People were finishing their meals. Everything came to her tinny and hard. She wanted to be cold a very long time that night and remember it, then bring that feeling back to California with her. Who knew when she would be back in New York again. Maybe never.

Her abuelita had wanted to feel winter hit her bones

too, and after an early dinner of ramen noodles, she had left for a walk while Monica was on the phone with her family. Freddy had won a baseball glove in the school raffle. Her mother had finally perfected lasagna, she hoped. Her father was concerned about the olive grove that had become infested with a disease.

"Xylella," he explained. The way it rolled off his tongue made it sound so lovely, though it was a terrible bacteria spread by spittlebugs. "It attacks the hearts of the trees first," he said. "Kills them slowly from the inside."

If not caught early enough, it would spread to all the trees in the grove, and they would need to be dug up and destroyed. The olive trees were old and knotty and beautiful. Like a whole forest of frozen wizards and witches.

"But Kita, thank goodness we caught it quickly. There are already signs of life," he assured her.

She did not bother telling them about Tabitha's return. It was all too fresh anyway. And she forgot to tell them what winter felt like, and her desire to experience a snowstorm. What the growing intensity of cold might feel like if she had the chance to stay longer. She meant to tell them that Amanda had been an excellent tutor these past two weeks, but she forgot. That would have made her parents happy.

There was a quiet knock on Monica's hotel-room door.

It was so quiet Monica mistook it for the neighbors on the other side of the thin walls. New neighbors came and went, each with their own sounds and habits.

The knock came again, louder. No one but the cleaning service ever knocked on their door, and it was far too late for that. Maybe her abuelita had forgotten her key. Maybe it was the owner of the mysterious key. She crept over to the peephole.

Through the tiny hole, she saw April standing there with a pillow, a sleeping bag, and a bag of popcorn. Monica slowly unlatched the door.

"Thought we'd hang out on your balcony together," April said, raising the bag of popcorn.

Instead of responding, Monica felt her shoulders collapse and tears roll down her face. April threw down her things and hugged her. "I'm sorry, Monica. I'm so sorry."

"I don't know why I'm crying. I knew I was coming to New York as an understudy. I shouldn't have expected anything more." Monica wiped her eyes. "Why are you here? Shouldn't you be at home resting up for rehearsal?" she added.

"Your grandma once said I could sleep over anytime. Is tonight okay?" Looking around the room, she added, "I don't mind the floor."

Her sour expression said otherwise. Monica laughed through tears.

"No one knew Tabitha was coming back, not even Artie," April said.

"I don't want to talk about it." Monica went over to the window and looked out at the bricks in front of her. "My abuelita put her life savings into this trip." Monica turned back around and studied the small hotel room. For the first time, she realized what a luxury it was. "April, I know how to break the curse. Well, mostly."

"What?"

"I started to tell you, but then . . . Tabitha, and I forgot." She went over to her backpack to get the file on the Ogden, but her abuelita walked through the door.

"Hi, Abuelita!" Monica said, picking up her backpack.

"Are you leaving?" her abuelita asked.

"Yes. April and I have to go to the theater for a little bit. April forgot something in her dressing room."

"Well, don't let me stop you girls. But hurry back. It's getting late."

They called Relly on their way to the theater. There was loud yelling on the other end.

"Where are you?" April asked, screaming into the phone.

"Hudson and I are at tae kwon do lessons," Relly explained.

"Can you both get away and come to the Ethel Merman after?" April asked.

"It's urgent!" Monica said leaning into the phone.

"Yeah. We'll be done by eight."

The kids gathered in a tight circle on the stage. The theater was empty.

Monica switched off the ghost light and began in a deep voice, "Dark forces come from the breath of the angry, the jealous, the greedy." The kids' eyes got wide. "But they also come from places of fear. . . ." She turned the ghost light back on and looked at the other three. "Sorry, that even scared me a little."

Hudson let out a nervous chuckle.

"The story begins here," Monica said, pointing to the stage, "with the Ogden family."

"The Ogden family. . ." Hudson said. "Rings a bell."

"Yes. They owned the Ethel Merman Theater for many decades. Long before it was called the Ethel Merman."

"The Ogden Theater!" April said. "I've heard stories about it. I never made the connection. That's *this* theater?"

"Aha! That's why we couldn't find anything in the Ethel Merman's file at the library before the 1990s, because it was all filed under a different name!" Relly smiled.

"Good detective work," April said.

"When Franklin Ogden died, he left the theater to his two children—twins, a son and a daughter, Henry and Hildy. Henry wanted to bring in big new shows with the greatest performers. He wanted what was popular and would sell tickets. They were glitzy and wonderfully successful." Monica paused. "Hildy, on the other hand, wanted to bring experimental, never-heard-of shows that were riskier. Smaller. She didn't care if they flopped—she wanted to attract new audiences with shows they could afford so they would get to know Broadway."

Monica stopped. She felt dizzy. It had been an exhausting day.

"And . . . ," Hudson said.

"They were always fighting about what shows to bring to the theater. Big and glitzy or small and unknown. Henry usually got his way. But one day, Hildy went to her brother and said she had an idea for a show. She would only need one night of space in the theater. Hesitantly, he said yes. Who would come watch her silly one-night show anyway? He was busy getting ready to bring a big new show to the theater from Europe. It was all anybody was talking about—the next big Ogden show—so what would her one night and one little show hurt?"

Monica paused again. The wind outside started to howl. A chorus of wind.

"The night of her show, the stage was empty but for one piano. Earlier in the week, Hildy had gone to every dance and music studio, performing arts school, and artist coop she could think of, throughout every section of the city, inviting artists to the theater. 'Come show off your talents and be a part of Broadway!' she said. The place was packed that night. Standing room only. But all those people"—Monica held in a breath, then continued—"none of them had ever performed on Broadway before.

"That night, she told the audience they were going to make their own production, tell their stories, and write a song. One after another, people got up onstage and started to talk or dance or sing their own original songs. How they'd come to New York from small towns. How they were looking for their dreams. People who had never acted told of their fears and worries. They had no voice in this world. They felt invisible. They shared their deepest, darkest emotions."

April dropped her head. It was not what she'd been expecting to hear.

"Together the audience wrote the lyrics, which Hildy, who was an amazing piano player and songwriter, one of the best on Broadway, set to music. When it was time to perform the song, she looked out into the audience for a volunteer. She pointed to a young girl, about our age. 'Can you read music?' Hildy asked her.

"The young girl said she could read a little music. It was a complicated piece. But her voice was beautiful. Like an angel. So beautiful that as she was singing, everyone in the audience started to cry. She started to cry. Hildy started to cry. Even the doorman started to cry . . . he blamed it on the onions in his sandwich."

"Jimmy Onions!" the three said. Monica smiled.

"When Henry saw what was happening in his theater, he was furious and stormed onstage. 'This is not what people want! People want to be entertained! They want to laugh. They come to escape from their problems; they don't want to be reminded of them!' He ripped the music from the piano and told everyone to leave immediately. The show was over. That night, there was a terrible thunderstorm. Lightning struck the Ogden, setting off all the sprinklers in the building. The theater was crying. The place flooded. It made Henry even more furious. He told Hildy she had cursed the theater. 'Leave and never return!' When she asked for the sheet music to the song, he threw her out.

"Many months later, theater critics reported that the Ogden audience had composed 'the most beautiful piece of music ever sung!' But Henry had already destroyed it. For many months after that, he tried to bring big shows to the theater. But they all flopped. Then he tried only comedies. But the theater kept crying. He brought in Ethel Merman, his favorite actor, to rechristen it, give it a new name, a new life. But it was too late. The cursed theater had been consumed by sadness and left to feed off fear."

"So what happened to Henry?" April asked.

"He ended up moving to Europe," Monica answered.

"What happened to Hildy?" April asked again.

"The papers never said."

"And here we are," Hudson said.

"So what do we do?" Relly asked.

Monica took her abuelita's shawl out of her backpack and wrapped it around herself. "Here," she said, pulling out four Coca-Cola cans from her bag. "First we drink these." She handed each one of them a Coke.

They looked confused.

"We must burp up any evil spirits we have inside ourselves before we begin."

The four kids laughed, and then chugged and burped several times.

"Then," she said, "if you have a good-luck charm, rub it now."

April rubbed her special bracelet. Relly pulled out his lucky lock of hair. It was his father's hair. They looked at Hudson.

"Fine . . ." He pulled up a cuff on his pants and rubbed his lucky green squirrel socks.

Monica rubbed her elephant necklace.

"Now, a protector. Every village, every cave, and every theater has its protector. That's us."

"Why us?" Relly asked.

"Because we don't fear the curse anymore," Monica said.

The kids nodded.

"Now what?" Hudson asked.

"Every cursed place has a spot that holds its secrets," Monica whispered.

"What does that even mean?"

"I'm not sure. My abuelita said we'd know it when we saw it."

No one had a clue.

"Maybe it's right here," April said.

The stage of the theater was where the original song was performed.

"Maybe, but people have fallen from the stage, so maybe not," Monica concluded.

"Artie's office?" Relly wondered.

It was a good guess. Maybe they'd feel whatever power they were supposed to feel when they unlocked the door.

Relly turned on his flashlight. The others used their phones for light. Their search began.

They raced to Artie's office, which was on the third floor. It was locked. Relly tried every tool in his backpack. Nothing.

"Now what?" April said.

"I've got it!" Hudson said. "Artie's office is right above the stage. There's a small window I've seen him look out of. Maybe it's open and we can get in that way."

The only way to get to the small window of Artie's office was to climb the catwalk above the stage.

"That's like a million feet up!" Relly said. Then he added, "And a million feet long! And did I mention I'm afraid of heights?"

"This is our trust fall," April said. "Like Miss Susan was talking about when we did our improv. We have to conquer our fears together."

They went back to the stage and began their ascent of the narrow ladder.

"It's amazing how high it is up here!" April laughed nervously as she made her way up first. The others followed slowly.

Then the lights attached to the catwalk started to flicker.

"Oh no, Ethel! Don't do this to us now!" Relly's voice shook.

The structure they were climbing toward started to sway. And there was a grumbling coming from the waterfall below.

"Don't look down, don't look down, just keep going," Relly repeated to himself.

But at that point, *down* was cloaked in darkness.

"Don't look up, either," Hudson said.

A few pails tied to the catwalk rattled.

The catwalk was only a couple of feet wide. Darkness meant they had to feel their way across by crawling.

April reached the window first, then flicked on her phone for light. "Want the good news or the bad news first?"

"Good news, please, good news," Relly said from the back, clinging to the platform for dear life.

"Good news is the window to Artie's office is unlocked," April said.

"What's the bad news?" Hudson asked.

"Bad news is it might be a tight squeeze."

"Oh man!" Hudson said, sizing up the window. "I hate tight places."

The other three managed to slide their way in, but Hudson had a tough time. When the waterfall below started to gurgle loudly and the catwalk started to shake harder, he blew out all the air he could while the other three pulled him through. They made it!

Artie's office was silent. It smelled like a combination of stale takeout and old coffee.

"It doesn't *feel* like anything powerful is here but clutter," April said.

"Look," Relly said. There was a whole stack of newspaper clippings on Artie's desk about the Ogden Theater.

Every headline, every flop. Stories about Hildy and Henry. About the night the theater was cursed.

"Wait . . . look." Hudson pointed to one of the newspaper articles.

In a blurry photo, a young Artie was standing next to Henry and Hildy in the theater.

"Artie's cousins. That's why he's been trying to save the Ethel Merman!" Monica said. Even she hadn't seen that one coming.

Relly took photos of the newspaper clippings.

"There's another storm brewing," Hudson said. They could hear the wind howling outside the theater. They were relieved that they could get out through Artie's office door and not have to go back the way they came. But somehow the dark hallway was just as scary. They looked behind them as they continued searching for what they did not know. They could not quit now.

They heard movement. It was the evening doorman checking around. "Kids, you in here?" He went one way; they went another.

Soon they found themselves back onstage. They moved deeper into the main auditorium. They tiptoed up the center aisle, touching row after row of empty seats.

Hudson whispered, "Why do you think the insides of so many theaters are red?" April looked around. How many theaters had she been in and never once thought about it?

"Such an astute observation," Relly said, quoting one of his lines from the show in the voice of his character, Pax. "Red," he answered, "is the first color to get lost in the dark. When the lights go down, red disappears."

"Not black?" Even April was surprised by this answer.

"Black shows dust and lint," Relly said, stopping to look around. "Theaters get dirty." He scratched his head. "Huh. So many people in one place night after night. Amazing more strangeness doesn't happen."

They reached the top of the aisle and turned around to face the stage. Their perspective changed. Once actors, now viewers. Everyone was lost in thought.

Hudson slapped his head. "I know where it is."

"Where?" They looked at Hudson with surprise.

"Amanda, that's pretty good . . . ," he said, chuckling to himself. "The classroom." He shrugged.

"The classroom!" Monica and April said together.

"The classroom?" Relly said.

"It's completely obvious, isn't it?" Hudson laughed.

"You're right!" Relly snapped his fingers. "In every good mystery it's always the least likely place."

"Why not?" April shrugged her shoulders. They had nothing to lose.

The lights flickered, and a door in the distance slammed

shut as they walked back down the aisle toward the empty stage, the ghost light their only source of light. A police car with its sirens going sped by outside.

A loud howling occurred.

Then a rumbling. Pipes! The waterfall onstage started to shake.

"Monica!" She heard Hudson call to her. He pulled her toward a side door, and they moved from fast walking to running. As they sped toward the classroom, papers from scripts and musical scores churned through the air. The piano in Studio A started to play. The wind outside now sounded like a woman hissing.

As they got closer to the classroom, the wind became visible in the theater, like tufts of clouds passing through walls.

Find it, Monica heard Jimmy whispering in her mind.

The theater started to groan.

"This is it," Hudson said in a loud voice.

The classroom door was wide open, and the lights were on, which surprised them. Wind and papers and costumes on hangers, rolling buckets, wigs, and duct tape were chasing behind them, caught in a tornado of energy.

"Go faster!" April screamed.

They made it into the classroom and slammed the door. All four leaned against it.

The room was still. As if nothing were happening on the other side.

"This is the center," Relly said.

"What now? There's nothing in here but chairs, a table, and a rubber chicken," April said.

"Think about our clues," Relly said.

"What clues? A key to a box with a message that says 'Happy Birthday'? *What clues?*" Hudson said, beads of sweat rolling down his face.

April let out a little whimper. Everybody looked at her. "If there are no clues, then we have to go back out there. And *out there* is really scary right now."

"Don't worry, April; we'll figure this out," Relly said confidently. "Somehow."

All of a sudden, the entire room started to shake. They held on to the door; then they held on to one another. It felt like an earthquake, rumbling below and above. The walls shook so hard, the dry-erase board came off one hook and fell at a diagonal, crashing to the floor and splitting like lightning had struck it.

They all stood in disbelief, not because the dry-erase board had come down with such thunderous force, but because after its fall, a portion of the wall was exposed, revealing a metal square the size of a large flat-screen television.

"It's a safe!" Relly exclaimed. And not a small one either, but a very large and old-looking safe. The kind that an olden-days bank robber would want to get his hands on, with a twisty dial to open it.

"No way. That thing's a vault!" Hudson said.

"It was right in front of us the whole time!" April laughed.

Whatever was inside, the kids were sure it was the answer to breaking the curse.

With the theater still quaking, they had to think quickly.

"Relly, our clues," Monica said. "'Happy Birthday'? What does that mean?"

"Whose birthday?" Hudson said.

"Let's go through the list of possibilities. Relly, what's Ethel Merman's birthday?" Monica looked at him with determination. He was holding his notebook.

He flipped a few pages in: "Born January sixteenth, 1908."

"Okay, let's try one-sixteen-nineteen-eight, or maybe one-sixteen-eight . . . ," Monica said.

"One, for January." Hudson twisted right to the number 1.

"Sixteen, for the day." He twisted left to the 16.

"Nineteen." He twisted right to the 19.

"Final number, eight." Hudson twisted left to the 8.

Nothing.

They tried it again with 1-16-8. Nothing.

They leaned against the table and studied the safe.

April had a thought: "Relly, pull out those old newspaper clippings about the Ogden. Is there anything about a birthday?"

Nothing.

They looked at any dates that stuck out.

Nothing.

"Wait! Look at this," Relly pointed out. "Hildy and Henry's birthday is November eighteenth, 1961."

"November eighteenth is the same day as our opening night!" Monica said.

That was it. 11-18-61.

Hudson turned the combination to the first number.

The room started to shake even harder, and the door started to shake as theater objects piled up on the other side.

"Hurry, Hudson!" April yelled.

He messed up and started over.

"Go slowly," Monica corrected. She put a gentle hand on his shoulder.

11 . . . 18 . . . 61.

Click.

The moment it clicked, the theater went calm.

Slowly, Hudson pushed down the heavy handle.

It opened.

"It opened!" Hudson laughed.

"It opened!" the others said in amazement.

"What's inside?" Relly and the others moved closer.

Inside was sheet music so old, so yellowed, and so badly water-stained that only a few stanzas could be made out, with large gaps of smudging in between.

The kids stood, wide-eyed, not knowing if this was a good discovery or a bad one.

Seven days until opening night

"We might be able to pull this thing off!" Artie announced, clapping. A preview performance the night before had brought in a few positive reviews from theater critics, who told Artie their thoughts privately. ("Captivating!" "Endlessly surprising!" "These kids bring it!") The curse had become silent the final days before opening night—eerily silent or delightfully silent, depending on who you talked to. "Your solo was brilliant yesterday, Relly! Just brilliant. Waterfall scene. Spectacular."

Monica rehearsed with the understudies. She tried not to show how much Tabitha's return bothered her. When the understudies weren't rehearsing, she would sneak to the back of the auditorium and watch her friends rehearse.

That day, Artie called up to her, "Monica, come down here and sit with me."

She sank into the velvety red auditorium chair next to him and watched the leads go through the last two scenes. Maria kept starting and stopping the music, hammering away at little details based on comments offered by the creative team during previews.

"Once the final tweaks are made, the show is 'frozen' until opening night. Meaning that that's it for any changes," Artie explained to Monica.

"Does this blocking look right?" Tabitha called onstage.

"No, no," Maria huffed, and pulled her a couple of inches to the left. "Here!"

"Maria's got a heart of gold, you know," Artie chuckled. "She could choreograph the song from an auto-insurance ad and make it interesting."

Monica turned to him and smiled.

Artie flipped a page in the script as he followed along with Maria. He crossed out a note and wrote a new note above it. Highlights in every color of the rainbow covered the page.

"How do you write music?" Monica asked.

Artie had written all the music for *Our Time*.

He raised the large legal pad that sat under the script, pointed to a page full of notes, then pointed to his head.

"And personal experience," he said.

She half nodded.

"Did that answer not satisfy you?"

"Well, not really."

He laughed. He actually had a quirky, fun, avuncular quality that Monica hadn't recognized before.

"Ever read poetry?"

"Yes, a lot of poetry," Monica said.

"Do you know what rhyming sonnets are?"

She did.

"Start there. Get your lyrics down as you pull in melody. Figure out what inspires you."

Monica closed her eyes and thought of what inspired her. She smiled. Artie studied her. They sat in silence. A switch in tempo onstage made Monica open her eyes.

They both turned their attention back to the stage.

"See how April's voice changes ever so slightly to almost become the pirate? Not overwhelming, just in hints."

Monica listened for it. "Yeah, I hear it now."

"Do you want to know something?" Artie asked with a smile before continuing. "I have five sisters." He paused, still looking at the actors onstage. "They were all very determined. Just like you."

Monica blushed.

"I was the only one who really had a passion for the theater. Funny thing is, I never learned how to play an instrument. Do you know how to play an instrument?"

She shook her head.

"Find someone who does. If you're interested in writing music, it will come faster. I learned to write music on my own. I could have been producing shows in my twenties had I worked with people who knew what they were doing instead of trying to do it all myself."

He scratched his chin.

"Tomorrow afternoon I have tickets to a charity concert at the Museum of Natural History. I can't make it. Would you and your abuelita like to go?"

Monica lifted in her seat. "Yes!" She hadn't been beyond the Ethel Merman for an afternoon of fun since she arrived.

The next day, Monica wrapped up rehearsal early with Artie's permission, and she and her abuelita walked through Central Park to the Museum of Natural History, an autumn chill pushing through the trees. The main hall where the concert took place was grand. "This would be a great place to ride a scooter," Monica's abuelita said in awe. Chairs in a dozen straight rows faced five seated musicians—two violinists, two violists, and a cellist. There were no seats left when they arrived, so they stood to the side next to the large T. rex, one of several dinosaur skeletons that loomed large in the massive hall. The room felt both old and new, strange and familiar. The quintet performed with scrupulous matching bow strokes. In perfect tempo they played a sunny kind of classical piece. Her abuelita studied the program that the attendant had handed her when they walked in.

"Mozart's String Quintet in C, K. 515," her abuelita whispered, as if this were obvious.

Monica leaned back against the waist-high wall that encased the dinosaur display to listen. A crowd closed in around them as more people gathered. For such a large space, it felt warm and intimate.

"You'll get yelled at for having your hand beyond the rope," a friendly, familiar voice said softly.

It was Amanda.

"Nice to see you're enjoying a slice of New York finally," she said, then turned to watch the performers. Though the musicians were seated, their bodies were lively and seemed to be in constant motion. They wore black dresses and tuxedos. Women in the audience wore fancy, stylish outfits; men wore suits with ties. Monica felt underdressed in the nicest tan pants she had brought, and one of her favorite pink sweaters.

After the performance, they toured the great hall with Amanda, who, unsurprisingly, knew every stone and speck of history about the place.

"This is one of my favorite museums in New York City."

She pointed to one of several quotes displayed on the wall. "'Keep your eyes on the stars and keep your feet on the ground.' Isn't that lovely? Theodore Roosevelt said that. This room is named after him: the Theodore Roosevelt Rotunda. Grand! Just grand! Ceilings soar to one hundred feet tall."

Later, the three of them walked outside where the air was calm and refreshing. They decided to share a cab. Amanda lived in the East Village, in a cozy one-room studio with her cat, Dolly, so she would be dropped off last.

They bumped along as their cab driver honked at another driver holding up traffic. Monica's abuelita, who sat in the front seat with the driver, didn't seem to notice the delay or the driver's growing impatience. She kept right on talking to the driver.

"I heard you were going to be at the concert tonight," Amanda confessed to Monica in the back seat. "Artie gave me an extra ticket as well."

"Oh!" Monica was surprised by this.

Amanda continued, "Did you know that Mozart wrote his first string quartet when he was only sixteen years old?" She smiled out the window. "Isn't it remarkable when you think about music? In one line, you can start off as gentle as a hummingbird and hit full throttle like an asteroid by the end! Just amazing when you think about it. I can't think of anything else in the world that can do that. Can you?"

Monica couldn't.

Back at the hotel room, Monica sat in one of the small chairs that went with the table and studied the sheet music they'd found in the vault. She'd studied it for four days, wondering what clues it had to offer, but this time, she saw it differently. Faded notes danced and played on the page in a way they hadn't before. Monica knew she was holding the real key to saving the Ethel Merman.

Thirteen

THE DAY OF OPENING NIGHT

All right, all right! Ladies and gentlemen," Artie said, entering the stage, where the full cast had formed a circle. The cast and crew started to clap and cheer and hoot.

Next to Artie was a stout, affable-looking man.

"Everyone, this is Mr. George from the Actors' Equity Association." Artie waved his hand toward the smiling man and stepped back.

The actors clapped loudly.

The stout man stood in the center of the circle.

"Thank you, thank you everyone. *Our Time* cast and crew," Mr. George said, smiling.

More applause.

He continued, "On behalf of the Actors' Equity Association, I'm here to welcome all of you to the Legacy Robe ceremony for opening night, on Broadway, of—drum roll—*Our Time!*"

Everyone erupted in applause. A photographer went around the stage taking pictures. April smiled ear to ear. Relly and Hudson stood on either side of her.

"Now, the Legacy Robe ceremony is one of Broadway's oldest backstage traditions, and it is honored by the Actors' Equity Association. It is a ceremony that both acknowledges and celebrates the actors working hard to made this musical come alive on Broadway.

"We'd like to invite all those actors making their Broadway debut into the center of the circle."

Relly ran into the center of the circle along with three adult actors. The photographer took their photo, and everyone clapped. "Wow, this is pretty awesome!" Relly laughed. The adult actors laughed with him.

"Now, in attendance today," Mr. George continued, "we have your director, Artie Hoffman, and his crew, who have worked so hard to get everyone to this point today. A round of applause for the crew."

More cheers.

"Next, I would like everyone who has received a robe in the past to come to the middle."

Tabitha proudly went to the middle of the circle and took a bow along with a few adult actors. "Thank you, thank you!" she said, graciously waving her arms to applause. Tabitha had received the Legacy Robe for her role in *Beauty and the Beast* a year earlier. But today was not her moment in the spotlight.

"And so it is time . . ."

The lights onstage began to flicker.

The actors looked at one another, but Mr. George only paused briefly and then continued, "I have the greatest pleasure of all time to announce this show's Legacy Robe recipient—he looked around the stage—"Miss April DaSilva!" The circle of cast members clapped and hooted loudly. Relly gave her a big hug. "I knew it!" He smiled.

A gust of wind blew a door closed with a loud slam backstage. Cast members looked around, but April waved and bowed with a big, grand sweeping movement. Nothing was going to dampen her moment. Especially not a curse.

"Miss April, please come to the middle of the circle."

Mr. George lifted the robe and opened it for all to see its details. It was a patchwork of designs from the different shows the robe had been passed to: *Miss Saigon*; *Hello, Dolly!*; *Jesus Christ Superstar*; *A Chorus Line*; *Wicked*; *Hamilton*. They all made up this robe's story, and now April was part of it. When she put on the robe, it was so big on her that her hands weren't visible through the sleeves and the entire bottom half dragged on the floor. The cast laughed at this and cheered.

"Thank you, everyone! It is such an honor to be here among your brilliance. And thank you, thank you, thank you so much for letting me be on this stage, sharing in the telling of this marvelous story. I am in the presence of such incredible minds," April declared.

The cast clapped some more. April had waited her whole life for this moment.

"You know, sometimes we forget. We just forget. We are so busy doing our thing and getting our work done that we don't stop to think how very lucky we all are to be on Broadway, doing a job we love doing." April had tears in her eyes.

Everyone nodded in agreement.

She shimmied her arms through the robe so they were visible, then continued. "The ritual of the Legacy Robe started in 1950, when an actor named Bill Bradley persuaded his fellow actor Florence Baum to let him have her dressing gown. He wore it for luck on opening night. He then passed the gown to an actor at the Imperial Theatre on their opening night, saying the robe would 'bless their show.' Then a rose from one of Ethel Merman's gowns—yes, *our* Ethel Merman—was attached, and the robe was sent on to another show."

Hudson leaned over to Relly. "How does she know all this stuff?"

"Because she's April. She knows all this stuff," Relly said in a whisper.

April continued, "The robe kept getting sent on to other opening nights, and soon enough the ritual was established. And so began the tradition of Broadway's Legacy Robe ceremony. Now I wear the robe, and per tradition, I am to circle the stage counterclockwise three times, and everyone touches the robe." The cast clapped eagerly.

"After that," April continued, "the recipient of the robe shall visit all the dressing rooms and announce, 'The show is blessed!'"

Everyone clapped again, and with that she circled around three times, counterclockwise, high-fiving cast members as they all hollered, "Brava!"

A thin beam of sunset stretched into the hotel room. Out came Monica from the bathroom with her hair in tight curls and dramatic eyes with a little sparkly eye shadow. She wore a semiformal black satin knee-length dress—the only dress she had packed, the only semiformal dress she owned, really. She noticed only after she put it on that it had an egg-sized chocolate stain smack-dab in the middle of the skirt from the last time she had worn it. It didn't matter, she thought—she would be hidden backstage with the other understudies in a small room, watching the show on a tiny TV monitor.

Her phone rang. It was Marissa, on FaceTime.

"Let me see you," Marissa said. Her usually long curly hair had been chopped very short.

"Your hair! You cut it!" Monica said in surprise.

"Yeah! I just felt like a big change! So my mom helped me cut it really short."

Monica laughed.

"Wow! You look amazing!" Marissa said.

Monica stuck out her tongue and then smiled. "Thank you. I'll look great for backstage."

"Are you worried about the curse?" Marissa asked.

"Ha! I'd rather talk about your new haircut," Monica said, leaning into the phone. "Show me the back."

Marissa angled the phone. "Guess who wanted to see my new do first?"

They both said the answer at the same time: "Freddy!"

"He kept telling me how next time, he would help Mom give me a 'fresh cut.'" This made Monica laugh hard. Marissa was like a second sister to Freddy; Monica could imagine the scene.

"Have you talked to your family lately?" Marissa's tone changed.

"Just a little bit ago. They couldn't talk. They were in a hurry. I guess they needed to do something at the farm. Why? Is there something wrong?" Monica felt an immediate wave of panic come over her. Were they not telling her something? Her mother *had* seemed a little strange over the phone.

"No, nothing's wrong. Nothing at all! I just saw Freddy yesterday. He was his usual wild self. He'd caught a bat and was racing around with it in a shoebox showing everyone."

"Oh!" Monica could always trust Marissa. This made her feel relieved.

"Come, Kita. I want to get to my seat early. I don't like to feel rushed," her abuelita said.

"I have to go, M.," Monica said.

"Well, I just wanted to say break a leg. Actually, I hope Tabitha breaks a leg," Marissa said, and then hugged her phone. "Love you, Mo!"

"Love you too. I'll call you after the show."

Her abuelita was waiting by the door.

They each slipped on nice black gloves.

"When I woke up this morning, Kita, and took my walk around the block—which I've enjoyed so much, by the way . . . what a lovely and simple thing to do . . . take a walk around a city block . . ." Her abuelita reflected on that before continuing. "But this morning, I could still see stars out from the night before. Stars in the morning are a good sign, Kita. It means the universe is not sleeping. It's fully awake and paying attention."

They were greeted by a blast of cold air, which infused a sort of liveliness as they walked briskly to the theater with tight smiles.

The *Our Time* marquee dominated the entire block with its bright lights. Everything else fell into shadows. When Monica entered the stage door, Jimmy was in his usual spot. He offered her a magic trick. Monica wasn't in a hurry to get backstage and enjoyed the distraction.

Once she was backstage, the electricity of opening night was tangible. A mixture of cologne and hairspray filled the air. There was a great deal of laughing and hugging. People were fully dressed in gorgeous costumes. The set designers had worked up until the very end.

Amanda rushed toward her. "Oh, Monica, you look lovely!" Amanda handed her a grand bouquet of flowers. The most beautiful bouquet Monica had ever received. "These came for you earlier. I wanted to be sure you got them personally." Amanda smiled. "If you need me for *any* reason tonight, I'll be left stage." Amanda winked.

Monica nodded firmly. Maria swept by and offered

Maria a smile. She anticipated a hit tonight, and it carried her in the moment.

Monica finally took a look at the card that had come with the flowers. The bouquet was from Marissa. It made her both happy and sad that her best friend—and her parents and brother—couldn't be there She found a big empty plastic jug and placed the flowers in ever so carefully. They looked like they'd come directly from her garden back home: roses, peonies, lilies, and, Freddy's favorite, snapdragons. Summer felt long ago and far away.

In her new dressing room, which she shared with a few other understudies, she quietly pulled out a silver rectangular box from under her dressing table. Gino's shoes had arrived a few days earlier. She took them out, two little dovelike creations. She held them to her chest. They made her feel a bit like a fraud, since she wouldn't be performing in them, but they also made her feel like Cinderella. She smiled, remembering how excited Relly, April, and Hudson had been when the shoes arrived.

Fourteen

OPENING NIGHT

The audience is packed with kids!" April galloped into Hudson and Relly's dressing room, her hair matted down with bobby pins and netting as she waited for her turn in the wig room. The boys' dressing room always surprised her with how tidy it was. Fresh flowers, which had been arriving for actors all day, perfectly lined the windowsill.

The two faces she encountered were not so in order. Hudson cracked his knuckles. Relly, who was never able to keep still, paced the room like a colt ready to bolt from his stall.

"And theater critics are everywhere!" April danced the

first few steps of the opening number, "Come on," she encouraged.

"What do you bet everyone's come just to see the curse," Hudson said.

"Look, curse or no curse, we have to go on," April said matter-of-factly. "The reporters are barely even talking about the curse anymore. They *are* asking me about being the Legacy Robe recipient, though." She stopped to swoop and swoon. "I've died and gone to heaven!" Monica posted it with *#legacyrobe*.

"Why would the curse just go away?" Hudson said skeptically. "After thirty years, it just vanishes? Doesn't make sense."

"I hear what you're saying. We got on television, which was lucky. Tabitha's back, Hugh Lavender's here, tickets are sold out from now until June. But the curse is not gone; it's just gotten quieter as we got closer and closer to opening night," April said. "That's how these things work."

"They always work that way in the movies," Relly said. "You think everything's gonna be okay, and then *wham!* There's a creepy ax murderer waiting for you in the closet."

Hudson caught April studying him from beneath her brow. "Don't do this to me now, Hudson," she said.

"Look, I have family members who traveled all the way from India to be here tonight, and I don't know why my costume isn't fitting right." Hudson tugged at his costume, which did seem a size too small all of a sudden. "It feels like it's going to tear off my body. I just want everything to go smoothly."

"I'm worried about getting hiccups onstage. Happens when I get nervous," Relly said as he pulled in air to hold his breath, still pacing the room.

"We have forty-five minutes before the curtain goes up; let's keep it together," April said, her mood suddenly shifting in line with the boys' anxiety.

"You have a visitor!" Monica poked her head in. They were all glad to see her.

"Telegram for the kids." A stagehand leaned in, holding a small yellow envelope in his hand. Receiving a telegram the old-fashioned way was another tradition in the theater.

April reached for the telegram. "May I open it?" She waved the envelope in front of her face like a fan, batting her eyelashes, before she tore it open. Her eyes widened with surprise as she read; she hugged the telegram.

"I've never seen one of these before! Aren't these used by really old people?" Relly asked.

"Telegrams are literally the cutest form of communication," April said, and with that she pulled out her phone and took a photo of the old-fashioned typewriter font on the yellow note card. *#Everseenoneofthese?*

"April, tell us who it's from!" Hudson said impatiently.

"It's from Chris Columbus!" April said with a loud squeal.

Relly knew it. "A really really *really* old person!" he blurted out.

"No, not *that* Christopher Columbus. Chris Columbus, the writer of some of the biggest movies from the 1980s!"

"And also the director of the first Harry Potter movie," Hudson said in his best British accent.

"Well, what does it say?" Monica asked with equal giddiness. An important telegram might be just the thing to lighten the mood and calm their nerves.

"It says: 'Can't wait to hear the Squad show 'em how it's done! Break four legs, *Our Time* squad!'"

The kids jumped in a circle, and Monica felt perfectly comfortable joining in the excitement.

Then Tabitha entered. "It's nothing short of magic!" she said with a tight, sarcastic smile. "Now, let's focus, people. I can't have this thing be a flop. My entire career is riding on this."

A hush fell upon the Ethel Merman. The lights dimmed. Monica watched on a small television in a tiny backstage room.

Relly, April, Hudson, and Tabitha took their spots, their

heads bowed. They were in the living room, the set bare but for a couch, a chair, a lamp, and, in the corner, a piano. The music began, and April hit her cue, her voice strong:

"It's our time. . . ." She held the note as the three others echoed her: "It's our time. . . ." The lights angled at the stage rose as all four actors began dancing their first number.

"They look good," commented Jacob, Relly's understudy, who was standing next to Monica.

"It's our time, to show what we've got. . . . Yes, it's our time, to be what they're not." Then the whole orchestra played, and the lights onstage got brighter, revealing all the characters and the full set. The scene was a thrilling opening, and everything seemed perfectly in sync. Audience members looked on in awe at the set design and at the intricate, quick dance moves that the kids seemed to so effortlessly perform.

Monica smiled. It was going to be okay. But just as soon as she thought it, she caught a curious look that Hudson flashed April. Onstage, April mouthed something. And Hudson mouthed back, *Oh no, oh no.* April was puzzled, then gave him a look that said, *Whatever it is, no!*

But it was too late. His costume pants had ripped in the back, all the way down the middle to the backs of his knees. His dance moves got weird, like he was hopping on hot coals. He tried not to let the audience see his back side, which made it even more awkward. Relly caught on quickly and couldn't help but laugh. Once Relly started laughing, it was almost impossible to stop him. He missed his line: *Our adventures begin when we all meet in the back.* This was the big introduction to the living room scene. But without being fed that line, Tabitha stammered, "Yeah— yeah, meet at my house," which now didn't make sense. Hudson missed his line entirely too; April slapped her forehead. Relly stopped laughing and began to hiccup. Quiet laughter could be heard from the audience.

The show was so tightly choreographed that once one thing went wrong, it all unraveled. The orchestra got tied up and the laughs came even louder. The picture frames on the faux living room walls started to fall off and come crashing down. The orchestra stopped playing. The actors stopped acting. The lights stopped moving. Everything froze.

From the back, a low, steaming hum could be heard. It got louder and louder. The Ethel Merman's old pipe organ, its anger building, like a dragon awoken. Fog that was meant for act two started to rise from the stage floor. Tech crew scrambled to figure out if someone had inadvertently turned on the dry-ice machine. The kid actors shuffled around onstage and moved back behind the leg of the curtain. Audience members shifted in their seats.

Stagehands didn't know what to do. Artie, who watched from the wings, knew there was nothing to do but watch the curse unfold. Secretly, it excited him. The organ kept playing, faster now. People started to whisper. Was it safe? They got visibly stiff in their seats.

"Oh no! Stop!" Monica yelled at the TV monitor with great fury and spine-tingling authority. "Stop!" she yelled again. Then a crack of lightning came, loud and direct. The bolt hit the theater so hard that it appeared to have come straight through the roof and onto the organ, which started to sizzle and smoke. It stopped playing, and the entire theater went dark. The audience screamed.

"Is this part of the show?" an audience member called out.

"I can't see a thing!" shouted another person.

"It's the curse!" someone else yelled.

Tabitha ran offstage.

The three other kid actors stood frozen in place.

Silence.

For several seconds no one said a word. The packed theater was still. Some waited for something to happen; others waited hoping nothing would happen.

In the back studio, the monitors went dead, and the understudies sat in horror wondering what was going on out front. Amanda tapped Monica's shoulder and whispered, "They need you. Let's hurry." Amanda and Monica raced down the dark, empty hall. The entire theater, even backstage, felt frozen. Within seconds Monica and Amanda reached the wing of the stage.

Slowly they walked onstage. Amanda went to the piano on the set; Monica took center stage. The three kid actors faded back.

"Listen . . . ," Monica said with lovely clarity.

"Liiiiiisten . . . ," she repeated, stronger now.

There she was, pure confidence. In total darkness. On a Broadway stage in front of a full house on opening night. The curse present and powerful. Monica present and powerful.

Monica looked over to the piano and whispered, "Are you ready?"

A music-stand light turned on next to the piano onstage. "Ready!"

The audience hushed. The piano sounded an even chord, round and sweet. It was a striking contrast to the destruction. Artie instantly saw it as a gift and leaned in to listen with everyone else.

Monica began to sing.

"Standing here
Feel the light on my skin

I see myself

In a place I've never been

No longer scared

No longer alone

I am home

I am home

I am finally found

Finally free

Content and at peace from the wars

That have built up inside of me

I am finally found

By a wish that came true:

That someday I'd be finally found by you

Thought I'd lost my voice

But it was here all along

Just waiting for me

To discover my song

The tune is familiar

But the words feel new

And now I sing them for you

I sing them for you
I am finally found"

The essence of the song was hard to describe, other than to say it was deep-feeling and hazy. Warm and comfortable. Then a wonderous energy built as Monica's voice made a shift in mood from softly dreamy to an expanded quickness, in the most pleasant, crisp way. Amanda picked up in staccato to match Monica's voice. The words came like a pearl necklace, every note separated by a knot to hold it in place. Her voice soared and swooped with emotion, and as she stood, her lone dark shadow grew and grew onstage. The theater throbbed with drama. The entire audience sat, entranced, on the edge of their seats, and like Orpheus taming the wild beasts, Monica kept singing to the curse.

Her friends recognized the music and several lines of the song right away. They were from the missing score they'd found in the vault. Other notes and lyrics were Monica's own creation. Old Broadway, new Broadway. The entirety of it was mesmerizing. It embodied irrepressible optimism, joy, hope. When darkness comes, hold it, love it, learn to understand it. Let the darkness speak; don't shut it out. The audience listened in rapture. One could almost see that as she sang each line, she was bending the curse.

The theater started to moan as she held notes in quivering vibrato, curlicued melisma, past the vanishing point. This was *Our Time*. Stunning. Extraordinary. Perfect strangers held one another and wept.

Monica's voice got higher and higher until finally she hit the highest note of the song and held it . . . just like Ethel Merman. High C for sixteen straight bars. Edge-of-your-seat electricity! All the walls in the theater started to shake. The lights flickered; a cold wind ripped down the aisles; the twenty-thousand-beaded chandelier danced. Monica's arms flew in the air as she held the note even longer. The audience was in awe; the kid actors were in shock; a theater got swept away in emotion. And then she dipped down again to the last line, softly.

Listen.

No one clapped right away. No one spoke. People were stunned by what they had just witnessed. Until finally one loud critic in the audience exclaimed: "Best show of the year!"

"Yes, she is!" Monica's abuelita hooted and began to clap. The entire audience followed until the theater roared with applause.

The lights in the theater came back on. The stage was bright. From the stage's piano came Amanda, who was perspiring and elated and smiling ear to ear. She walked toward Monica and they hugged.

"Happy Birthday, Hildy," Monica whispered to Amanda. It was right in front of them, but they didn't make the connection like Monica did. She had promised Amanda earlier that she would keep Amanda's identity a secret. Why? Because, for now, Amanda liked her new, quieter life as a tutor. But she did promise Monica that maybe someday, Hildy would make a return to Broadway.

After Monica's performance, the theater settled into a calm. It almost seemed like the old cracks in the walls had instantly healed themselves and the musty smell had vanished. Even the chandelier shone brighter than before. The audience members started to chant, "We want *Our Time*! We want *Our Time*!" With very little convincing, Artie agreed to start the show over, with Monica playing Tony! The costume department quickly got Hudson a new pair of pants. Tabitha, still shaken and embarrassed, didn't complain.

Magic was made that night at the Ethel Merman. Their performance was flawless. Amazing, in fact. And a curse, which everyone had thought would be impossible to break, was broken. The kids bowed to a standing ovation and then almost collapsed in a huge group hug onstage. People called out "bravo" and "brava." Monica wanted to pinch herself. So she did.

As the lights went up, Monica heard a familiar voice calling, "Monica, Monica!"

Freddy was running down the center aisle. Was she seeing things? She wasn't seeing things! "Freddy!"

And right behind him were her parents.

"You're awesome! I can't believe you're my sister!" Freddy said, jumping on the stage and wrapping his little arms around her, followed by her father, who had tears in his eyes.

"How . . . who?" Monica said, half laughing, half crying.

"We couldn't miss opening night." Monica's mother gave her a long hug and a soft kiss on her forehead.

"And what an opening night it was! Broadway history in the making." Artie came over with a long, fast stride and shook Monica's parents' hands firmly and a little too enthusiastically. Freddy's, too. "Your sister is very proud of you," Artie said to Freddy. "I hear you want to be an astronaut one day."

"Yeah. And now that I have a sister who's a star, I'll definitely have to travel to outer space!"

The show's after-party was at the famed Al Joseph's restaurant. Famous for its meatballs and, well, its after-parties. Everyone dressed in their best outfits, and a press line greeted the actors and crew as they walked in.

"Al Joseph's! Never in my life!" Monica's abuelita said, and hugged an unsuspecting waiter, causing him to almost spill the two water glasses he was carrying. But before they got much farther in, Monica was surrounded by reporters. "Monica! Monica!"

"Let her through, people; let her through," April and Relly said, ushering Monica past the crowd. April pulled her aside. "Before you say anything to anyone with a note-pad or a tape recorder, here's what you need to know about giving an interview. Trust me, I learned the hard way. One: Talk, but don't talk too much. Two: Gesture with your hands. You know, it makes you look really passion-ate about your work. Like this. People love that. Three: Be humble. Never ever act like you knew the show would be a hit. Be almost surprised but not too surprised when they compliment you. Of course, while not saying too much and still using your hands . . ."

Hudson came over with a meatball on a toothpick. "They call these meatballs?" He shoved it into his mouth. "Mmm, actually, they are pretty good."

"You guys . . ." Monica's eyes were bright and warm. "We did it!"

"We did it!" they all said with a mix of joy and relief.

"But we still have to wait for the reviews to come in . . . ," April said nervously.

Relly was already scrolling on his phone. The reviews of a new show were always published during the after-party, and they could make or break a production. One bad review and the show could flop.

"Nothing yet," he said.

A few reporters came over and asked the group questions. Monica was careful not to talk too much. And she used her hands. And acted humble.

Amanda swirled over, beaming with joy. "You might want to know, your first review came out."

Relly pulled out his phone and scrolled immediately.

"Found it!" Relly read it to the group: "'Quirky young actors of *Our Time* steal the show . . . make light of their dark world . . . brim with talent . . . beamed onstage . . . spectacular . . . brilliant . . .'" He looked up at them and then continued: "'Broadway's must-see show of the year!'"

They formed a tight circle and hugged one another.

"Yes, yes, show of the year. Of course it is!" Artie said, coming over to congratulate them. "Was there ever any doubt? Ha!" Artie's brow was sweating.

There had been a whole lot of doubt. And fear. Fear will get you every time. Until you meet it face-to-face and decide fear is not who you are. Fear is not a theater or a curse or a legacy. It's just a feeling you get. The same as courage. It's just a choice.

In the end, it was Artie who had flown Monica's family out from California to New York City—with some begging from Monica's castmates. And it was Artie who had slipped Monica the key. Why? Because he saw a lot of himself in her, and he knew she wouldn't quit until she found the safe, uncovered the mystery and the story behind the Ethel Merman, and broke the curse. The one thing he didn't quite know was how the missing music would—or if it even could—break the curse, until he heard Monica sing.

And the sale of the Ethel Merman? Just a marketing stunt. The greedy developer who wants to buy a historic theater currently showcasing a musical about a greedy developer? *Brilliant.*

So it's true: there were a few monsters under the bed. Some of the things that happened at the Ethel Merman probably happened because of coincidence. People slam doors. Fires in wig rooms happen. Beams come crashing down under the weight of water. Actors trip and fall. Lights in old theaters flicker. A lot also has to do with the way you tell the story. Especially on Broadway.

Acknowledgments

The most important thing I have learned while working in the theater is that the show must go on no matter what . . . and putting up a memorable performance takes a Fearless Squad. I'm so grateful to the people who are part of mine.

I want to shine the spotlight on my grandma Marie Belle Carriere for sharing her love of theater and Broadway belters with me. My parents, Paul and Robin Gonzalez, first, for naming me after the Barry Manilow hit; second, for buying me a karaoke machine; and third, for carrying it anywhere and everywhere that someone would let me sing. My beautiful sister, Monica, who let me wear sequins and stand in the front to sing at all of her piano recitals. My brother, Anthony, for attending ALL of my performances growing up and for watching the movie *Annie* on laser disc with me hundreds of times.

Gracias a mis Abuelos por sacrificar tanto para darnos una vida meior.

Thank you to my guide, Brin Stevens. I knew from our first conversation at Joe Allen's, where I never stopped talking, that you would teach me so much and that we would never run out of things to talk about. Ever.

A big heartfelt thank-you to my agent, Jessica Regel, for believing in these characters and the magic of Broadway. Carey Albertine and Saira Rao at In This Together Media for encouraging and challenging me to go further.

My incredible editor, Alyson Heller, for your wisdom and dedication. Thank you, Karen Sherman, for your exquisite attention to the details. And thank you to Geraldine Rodriguez for creating an incredible book cover.

To the entire team at Aladdin. You guys are the best!

Thank you, Tom Kitt, for cowriting the song "Finally Found" with me! What a dream!

Thank you to my friend and confidant Lou D'Ambrosio for your endless support and encouragement and all that you do to help me soar.

Thank you, Sandy Jacobs, for believing in me all these years and helping to make so many things happen!

Thank you, Mark Bonchek, for being so generous with

ACKNOWLEDGMENTS

your wonderful mind and literally being there the very moment we created Fearless Squad.

Thank you to everyone in the Broadway community. From the producers, directors, casting directors, choreographers, designers, orchestrators, musicians, actors, stage crew, ushers, porters. I love you all.

To my best friend, Darrell (Relly) Grand Moultrie, for your integrity and honesty always. To my right hand (wo)man, Alexa D'Ambrosio, thank you for all you do.

To my husband, Douglas Melini, you are my rock and biggest motivator.

To my daughter, Maribelle, te quiero hasta la luna.

About the Author

Mandy Gonzalez possesses one of the most powerful and versatile contemporary voices of our time. Currently starring in the megahit *Hamilton* as Angelica Schuyler, Mandy also originated and starred as Nina Rosario in the Tony Award–winning Broadway musical *In the Heights*, for which she received a Drama Desk Award. Mandy also starred as Elphaba in the Broadway production of *Wicked*, blowing the roof off of New York City's Gershwin Theatre each night as she belted out the signature song, "Defying Gravity."

Mandy is a Warner Music artist and recently released her debut album, *Fearless*, which debuted at number thirteen on the iTunes pop charts. Mandy has performed with symphonies around the world and recently made her Carnegie Hall debut with the New York Pops.

ABOUT THE AUTHOR

Mandy is the proud founder of *#FearlessSquad*—a social media movement for inclusiveness and positivity. *#FearlessSquad* connects millions of people around the world, encourages them to be their best selves, and helps them empower one another.

Mandy is also an author—she recently published a widely cited article in the *Harvard Business Review* on how to overcome one's fear of public speaking and be more confident in communications and leadership.